Praise for OBJE

"Susan Finlay's deft, subtle novel examines the psychic texture of life through our relation to things... objects of all kinds, from Filet-O-Fish sandwiches to high art, Le Creuset cookware, bicycle baskets and purpose-built, modern flats. *Objektophilia* is witty and brisk and devastating all at the same time." Chris Kraus

"I love how it sees space, almost as a medium for objects to appear. There is a narrative, but it really does seem to exist as a way to 'exhibit' these objects. It's fascinating." Amina Cain, *The Paris Review*

A work of great richness and pleasure, as well as corresponding weariness and sarcasm [...] A lush exhibitor of objects [...] A beautiful reversal of all those novels whose fictional elements exist solely to advance the plot. *Times Literary Supplement*

"Susan Finlay's funny, bleak and sharply observed novel Objektophilia, about a London-based design critic and her architect historian partner, immerses us in the obsessive preoccupation with objects—artworks, buildings, fast food, luxury goods, 'niche' design—that besets those who make a living from the culture industry... Part erotic fixation, part cultural disease." *Art Review*

Susan Finlay

My Other Spruce and Maple Self

Moist

First published in 2021 by Moist
https://moistbooks.cargo.site

ISBN 978-1-913430-02-3
eBook ISBN 978-1-913430-03-0

A catalogue record for this book is available from the British Library

I

Leave

Obviously, my looks helped although not so much because of their quality as their type. The promotional photographs always adhered to the following formula: auburn waves and ivory shoulders, a dress in watered taffeta and the Montagnana between my thighs. Sometimes my eyes addressed the viewer directly while at others they disappeared beneath my lids in near orgasmic flicker but bar the cover for Haydn, in which I was temporarily reduced to black and white, these were, perhaps ironically, the only variations on a theme.

Yet as I contemplated my reflection framed and weighted by the same black wood as the examination table I noticed that many of the lines which, up until this point, had only been there when I laughed had now taken up permanent residence around my mouth and eyes. Upon receiving the dubious accolade 'Sexiest Classical Musician' I had been disparaging of it and yet the thought that I might no longer be the recipient of such praise, even if it did come via Gramophone Magazine, filled me with insurmountable grief . . .

"Ms Le Clef-"

"Allegra, please."

"Allegra."

The Consultant who was reassuringly dark and large—a tombstone almost—reached for my hand. In the background the cadmium flock burned with the same subdued emphasis as my curls did and in the foreground a sheaf of papers momentarily disrupted by our movements quivered.

"Now, we have two options - or two without any major risks. We can either replace the broken piece with a substitute or try a newer treatment whereby we stimulate the bone to make it grow-"

"But which is quicker?"

"Quicker . . .?"

He paused, removed the wrist-support then stroked the tender skin beneath. Instinctively my gaze shifted back to the mirror but this time my throat—too naked, too exposed—and the turquoise vein that ran unevenly across it.

I wrenched my hand away and snapped, "What I mean is, how long until I can play again?"

He took a small step backwards.

"Well, it's a slow process-"

"How slow?"

"Well . . . perhaps a year. Of course you'd have to build up to it. Maybe start with ten minute sessions-"

"But I need to practice for two hours a day. Minimum. Usually I do four. Often six."

"Well . . ."

"Two or four or six," and the hysteria that since the accident had begun to bubble up with increasing frequency now boiled over, "Two or four or six!"

"Ms- I mean to say Allegra. I understand that it's a shock-"

"Ideally six!"

"As I was saying-"

"As a student I did eight! What you're telling me is- is- is-" but still I couldn't breathe, "is that it is over!"

You or Him

The Consultant sat down on a leather chair the proportions of which was perfectly attuned to the size of his limbs. He drummed his fingers on the desktop and for the first time I noticed that the hair beneath his knuckles grew in tiny pubic swirls. Before he had appeared simply as a professional being with no discernible or individual features besides his overall scale and colour. Yet in noticing this one detail I now became aware of many others. The hair on top of his head which was coarse and would have also been unruly had it not been for the sheen of wax that held it back, the faint blue-black shadow that ran along the edges of his jaw, the almost feminine lashes . . . I pictured the swirls on his knuckles growing larger as they roamed across his chest, stomach and the so on that lay beneath his belt buckle, and then the so on growing larger too - then caught sight of the slightly tacky, soft-focus portrait of what I assumed must be his wife-

"Regardless of time I'd recommend the second treatment."

"A- a- a paper . . ."

"A paper?"

The Consultant looked at me confused and then as if suddenly understanding reached inside his desk and extracted a paper bag. Before he had time to unfold let alone offer it to me however I had already grabbed it from him and then pressed it against my mouth with an eagerness that even in the midst of passion would have been humiliating. I began to suck and as I did so my breathing slowed as did my thoughts, gradually detangling themselves from the instant that was myself and finally reconnecting with the wider world around me. I put down the bag and looked out of the window. The trees were completely still and the sky was a cloudless blue. I thought of Regent's Park which began at the end of the road and the perfectly manicured rose garden that resembled a china plate.

"That is, if you want the break to heal permanently," said the Consultant.

"Of course I want it to heal permanently."

A few more seconds passed and then he reached for the wrist-support. I felt the cold metal of his wedding ring graze the back of my hand followed by a tight, cramp like sensation as he rebound it.

The Swan

Verity Peach was waiting in reception. As soon as she saw us she dropped her yoga roll and bounded forward. The gesture was so guileless that I was reminded of our time at the Academy (or else a Labrador slobbering). Like the rest of our contemporaries her talent had never been anywhere close to mine. Yet she had never attempted to disprove this fact nor been upset by the offer of second flautist in a second-rate orchestra that she had taken up after finishing her studies. Rather she had greeted each circumstance in which she found herself with genuine enthusiasm and as if it had never occurred to her that she could and even should want more.

Over the years I had come to view these acceptances that were also choices in much the same way that I viewed her partner Hale, a man who as stupid and out-of-date as his diesel powered car; a vehicle so disgusting not to mention dangerous that like him it should have been destroyed. Of course my talent was at times a burden due to the continual devotion it required but so too was Verity's penchant for mediocrity. I remembered how embarrassed I had once been to see her shaking spittle from her flute, and even more so when she referred to it as a 'music shower' . . .

"So . . .?" she said, expectantly.

"So . . ." I began, but before I had time to go any further the receptionist turned the volume on the radio up.

The pitter-patter of Saint-Saëns fell down upon us and drowned out what had nearly been our conversation as well as the group of nurses gossiping at the room's far end. Judging by their expressions I concluded that one of their patients was about to die or worse still be permanently disfigured.

I took a deep breath and somewhat more loudly said, "So *he's*" and I nodded at the Consultant, "going to drill into me and stuff me with electrodes and then, a year or so after I've become a sort of walking science fiction, I might just possibly be able to hold a bow."

"Ms- Allegra . . ." he began.

"*Please*," finished Verity, "He isn't Ivan. And I'm sure he's doing everything he can to help. Perhaps if we tried some sort of juice cleanse . . ."

I heard but did not listen to her voice as it continued to expound upon the nature of my ailment and its fictitious relationship to vegetable purees just as I had seen but ignored the nurses. Instead, I became aware that Verity was wearing rainbow socks and that they matched the rainbow ribbon that held her yoga roll together. For a moment I wondered where one bought rainbow socks and then almost as briefly why, even though twenty years had passed since we had graduated from the Academy we were still, at forty-one years of age, 'best friends'. I was so often embarrassed by or even ashamed of her behaviour. Yet at the same time I felt a reluctant urge to protect her - a dynamic now further complicated by the fact that unlike me she had survived the accident unscathed.

I turned back to the Consultant and raising my voice above her's said, "Thank you for your time."

"Allegra-"

"Thank you for your time," I repeated, more forcefully.

"Allegra-"

"It's been an absolute pleasure, but as I'm sure you'll appreciate I have other things to be getting on with."

I grabbed hold of Verity and before either she or the Consultant could protest dragged her through both sets of double-doors. Once outside the surgery though I stopped and stood, motionless, at the top of the steps. There was something so unreal about the neat Georgian houses opposite and the laurel ball trees in front of them that once again I saw England as a piece of antique porcelain. As something no longer used or displayed due to its unfashionable appearance and propensity to crack . . . And then either incapable or perhaps unwilling to explain myself I started running.

The Others

Harley Street was sprinkled with women some of whom were wearing surgical strips across their noses. What I could see of their faces was neither young nor old – just rich.

"It's not what you have done," said the one nearest to me and her footsteps drew level with my own ones as having outrun Verity they now slowed, "but how you maintain it. Of course everyone has their specialty —face, breasts, labia—I had a different man for each . . ."

The woman next to her removed her sunglasses revealing a series of turquoise stitches tugging at the purple skin beneath them then reached inside her handbag and produced a magazine. The cover depicted two before and after photographs. Both were of the same tanned, white woman in a string bikini. In the before picture soft, doughy looking rolls of flesh splurged out from each of the Lycra triangles whereas in the after one her skin was stretched tight across her bones. The headline stated, 'From Blubber to Lover,' and then in slightly smaller writing, 'The Men Who Rebuilt Maxine' followed by a summary of the accompanying TV pull-out and guide to high-street fashions.

My mouth filled with an acrid taste. I spat it out and pretending not to hear the tutting noises that then ensued crossed over to the newsstand opposite. I glanced at the other very similar looking magazines before selecting a bottle of sparkling water. Straight away I opened it and started drinking and as the bubbles prickled against my cheek I looked up. A blue plaque commemorating an infamous psychoanalyst was positioned on the wall above me. For the first time that afternoon I thought of my husband Albion. Not in the removed, abstracted terms of those who like the Consultant shared his physical type but of my husband specifically. From our very first meeting I had been aware of how others would see us together (enviable, credible, photogenic . . .), but more importantly I had sensed his dominance, or the untapped potential for it. I could not have said why this was so besides the way he moved his hands and yet my musician's instincts had as usual proved correct. Looking at the plaque I recalled an occasion near the start of our relationship where he had suggested that we pick a safe word and how without thinking I'd said, 'Satan'.

The Messages

My handbag pinged. I took out my phone and read, *How did it go? Albion X.* And then, PING! *Doctors not referendum, Albion X.* PING! *So when do U think U will escape 2 Amsterdam? Albion X.* PING! *Or do U want me 2 fly back to U, pick U up & go together? Albion X.* PING! *Miss U beautiful X X X.*

I drank some more water. It had been over a month since Albion had arrived in the Netherlands and I had begun avoiding the question of at what point I would join him. When the Museum had made their offer I had still been well and it had been clear to both of us that he should accept it. I could play or not play my cello anywhere while he was eager for the chance to cement his career not as the specialist in British nineteenth-century painting that he had previously been known as, but as an important contemporary art expert the significance of which, beyond its significance to him, I did not fully understand. Consequently it was not thoughts of my own career that held me back but the fear of being seen for what I was without it. The accident had not only ruined our appearance on the outside but had also resulted in Albion making numerous attempts to be tender in private; an act requiring endurance on the part of the receiver that in this instance was tantamount to an acceptance of my own disgusting needs. I knew that on the surface my wish to avoid the Netherlands seemed selfish but at the same time that this was what I was. I had always had an innate fear of anything that could be described as running deep; a state of being that I equated with being in some way wounded.

The Circus

I carried on walking down Great Portland Street and towards Oxford Circus. A middle-aged man in very short shorts was standing on an upturned orange box.

In his right hand was a megaphone into which he shouted, "Shopping won't save you!" and then when nobody responded, "And sex won't either!"

A group of teenagers with pierced stomachs and candy-floss coloured hair surged past him. They smelled of hairspray, sweat, and cheap deodorant none of which made them any less attractive.

"Did you read the article?" said a narrow-hipped girl with a stone in her navel, "Apparently yesterday's most Googled phrase was what is the EU?"

"I think it's going to be okay though," said an equally ambiguous looking boy, who could have been her brother or her sister or some other intersex, alien twin, "there's an internet petition we can sign . . ."

They started snogging. The other teenagers carried on towards Niketown, knocking into them as they went along.

"Don't be a sinner, be a winner!" shouted the man on the orange box and then having used up all his slogans he returned to the beginning, "Shopping won't save you! And sex won't either!"

The snogging couple drew apart and the girl turned toward him.

"But our island is sinking!" she shouted back, "We're already fucked!"

The Swan

I took a right and headed into Mayfair. Arab girls with big hair and bigger handbags murmured into brand new iPhones while even bigger bodyguards walked behind them weighed down with boutique carrier bags. Arab man with fat ties and pointed shoes drank espressos at round bar tables, and red-white men in loafers but no socks haw-hawed like good old-fashioned Sloanes. A bedraggled barefoot figure approached a couple sat outside an Italian restaurant and asked for money. They shook their heads and then as soon as he left them raised their eyebrows at each other.

"Well really," said the woman, "he's got a nerve!" and then examining the menu, "Shall we get the Frascati? Seeing as we're having fish?"

Shall we get the Frascati? I repeated inwardly and thinking as I did so that of such things my life had until recently been made. Shall we stick with the Muscadet or try a white port with dessert? Will you take a babà with your coffee? They really are sensational . . . Again Saint-Saëns started playing although now it was not the actual music but the memory of *The Swan* that moved inside me and as the melody rippled through my body my broken hand began to twitch-

"Excuse me? Miss? Can I help you?" said a man in a top-hat.

I started then stared at him confused then looked back down at the wrist-support that was now peeking out from underneath the chiffon sleeve inside of which it had previously been hidden. I thought of Verity's yoga roll and the rainbow ribbon that had matched her socks. Of the Consultant, his wife and my husband. Of his face, my breasts, my labia, Frascati, Muscadet, white port and babàs – which really were sensational . . .

I struggled back towards the surface arched my neck and hissed, "No, because I'm helpless."

"Excuse me? Miss . . .?"

And as I glided past the doorman and into the hotel foyer I did so to the accompaniment of this strange white creature flailing.

Scarlett

It was not yet four but Scarlett was already on her second Szarlotka, a vodka and apple cocktail served in a highball glass or as I put it to myself three parts juice cleanse and so it followed good for me. As soon as my own one arrived I took a large gulp relishing the unwholesome taste as much as the Art Deco interior which, in light of the fact that it would not be long before my own body also belonged to the age of the machines, seemed especially soothing.

"So you managed to escape Pilates with the Peach?" said Scarlett and downed the remainder of her drink while also motioning to the barman that she required another, "She'll kill us all if she's not careful."

"But she genuinely believes that she can help the helpless," and I also took another glug. "It's why she and Hale are still together."

I fully expected Scarlett to laugh and make a harsher comment and for me to then feel guilty and try to put it right only on this occasion she appeared to have forgotten our routine. Instead she shrugged causing the silk straps of her camisole to slip down and reveal even more of her shoulders. Then she picked up her phone and pushed it towards me so that I could the screen, which displayed an erect penis. I didn't understand what the point of it was other than to reinforce my own comparative lack of virtue and much to my chagrin blushed.

"People just said them to me," she said.

"What sort of people?"

"People on tinder. I mean, they usually send a few messages first – work, sports, blah, blah, blah – and then they suggest that we move it to WhatsApp and then it's like 'Hey babez check this out!' "

"Lolz," I said flatly.

The barman placed a third Szarlotka on the table while clearly trying not to stare at Scarlett's phone and Scarlett drummed her nails, which were red and pointed, up and down on top of it. He waited as the nails tapped out each second then all of a sudden bolted, at which point Scarlett burst out laughing. Then almost immediately she frowned.

"Ever since I became a woman other women have warned me to be gentle," and I could tell from the way that her voice had moved to the back of her throat that her little teeth were clenched tight together, "told me that men are scared of being dismissed or laughed at. But I mean really, if you want someone to take you seriously" and just as quickly her expression changed again, only this time it switched to one that was jovial, "then why send them pictures of your penis?"

John and Johnnie

Two men with diamond earrings and huge fur-lined jackets which, in light of the heat, appeared both ostentatious and ridiculous entered the hotel bar. The older of the two also had a mole below his eye that fell in the shape of a tear so that if viewed from a distance one would have thought he'd been in prison. I watched as the one with the mole whispered something in the barman's ear then walked over to our table.

Looking not at me but at Scarlett he said, "I wanted to know just what it is you're drinking? It looks very . . ."

"Beguiling?" and in response she gave an even more revealing shrug, "I think that's a good word don't you?"

"I think it's an excellent word. But I doubt it's the name of your drink."

Scarlett laughed then ran her nails across the fur-lined edge of the man with the mole's jacket and the man with the mole laughed back. The sound was wolfish, masculine, unrepentant. I could see that inside of his mouth was very red and he was now so close to us that I could smell his breath which was tinged with Champagne.

"And your name is?" I said abruptly.

"Johnnie," he said, still laughing, and then motioned to his friend who made his way towards us, "and just to make things easy for you this here's John."

"A couple of Johns," I said in the same tone that I had said 'lolz' earlier.

"Yeah but I'm *Johnnie*," and then once more to Scarlett, "So what do you do? I'm sure it's terribly . . . *beguiling*."

"I'm a seamstress. And I make pretty dresses for pretty ladies at the Opera," she smiled quickly, apologetically, in my direction then continued in his, "and sometimes the orchestra," before then turning all of her attention to Johnnie's hood, "and sometimes if they're very pretty," and this time she shrugged so deeply that the lace tops of her bra showed, "then I also do the boys."

Rachmainoff's Sonata in G Major

"And what about you Allegra? What do you do?" said John.

"Oh . . . this and that."

I listened to the faint strains of Rachmaninoff were now emanating from behind the bar and tried to concentrate on them instead but then realising that something more was called for and not caring if I sounded irritating I said, "Tell me, how would you define The Romantic?"

"The Romantic, or just romance?"

"I don't know. Either. Both."

John appeared to consider my question and as he did so the barman returned with four glasses of champagne that I presumed Johnnie must have ordered prior to joining us. Yet they were not served in the usual flutes but the old fashioned type of glasses supposedly modelled on Marie-Antoinette's breasts. I reached for one of them and as I did so the image of a pink nipple pressed onto a wet, clay slab forced its way into mind-

"Romance?" I persisted shivering.

"Romance . . ." John repeated as the music's intensity increased.

"Romance," said Johnnie then paused dramatically as both the piano and the cello climaxed, "is the sacrifice of *my* dignity" and he took hold of Scarlett's hand and with an exaggerated flourish kissed it, "for *your* vanity."

Automatic Reply

I took out my phone. I wanted to reply to Albion but still couldn't see how Amsterdam would work if my body didn't. The hotel bar in which I was now seated was not dissimilar to the one where he and I first met. We had both been invited there in order to speak at an arts charity dinner and had of course offered our services for free on the implicit understanding that our cultural capital would increase as a result. Sure enough half a page in the *Evening Standard Magazine* had appeared the following Friday framed in such a way that we had dazzled dazzlingly together. We had been photographed against an array of paintings by Edward Burne-Jones, or alternatively against several flatter, lesser versions of myself . . .

Yet this Albion was no longer my England or indeed any other body consumed by grim self-hatred or pompous misplaced self-love. I closed my eyes and tried to imagine Amsterdam's Concertgebouw—its austere façade, high white walls, plush red seats—and then myself spot-lit upon the centre of the stage. I tried to imagine being once again admired and objectified—a word that had ever really bothered me, quite the opposite in fact—while at the same time trying to ignore the possibility that I might never have an audience either here or in the Netherlands, again . . .

I opened my eyes and typed *Appointment went well. Should have date 4 operation in next few days. Will let U no more soon as I do. Allegra X.* Then reached for the champagne.

The Celebrated Chop Waltz

We continued drinking for many hours meaning that it was past eleven when we finally arrived at Johnnie's. His apartment occupied the entire top floor of a shiny new-build block. A massive flatscreen television took the place of a fire and a solitary white orchid bowed with corporate grace across a black lacquered baby grand. The only other furniture that I could see was a grey modular sofa and an Arco floor lamp the curved spine of which mimicked the flower's. I sat down next to John who began to pat his pockets and then a moment later produced a bag filled with weed.

I said weakly, "I think I should be going."

"Oh for fuck's sake," said Scarlett, "it's not like you have work tomorrow."

"I know but . . ."

But nothing, because my talent was so far away from where I was now that it could no longer do me any harm, as was my husband-lover-torturer because how could any lover or even love ever cease to be a cause of hurt? Before the accident I would never have considered drinking to get drunk let alone taking drugs because my own self-punishing ways, my own gruelling practice schedule already took enough from me as it was, and because I was far too vain to indulge in anything that could have dented my abilities or the social standing that resulted from them - but now? I turned away from the door and headed back towards the piano.

Not knowing what else to do I pressed middle C and with some surprise said, "It's in tune."

"Do you play?" said Scarlett looking at Johnnie.

"Do I play?" said Johnnie looking at Scarlett.

Then he stood up also, and then made a great show of sitting down again at the piano stool while

Scarlett and John twisted round to watch. As soon as he was sure that he had everyone's attention he cracked his knuckles, placed his index fingers on F and G and hit them each six times. Then he moved the left one to E. Then to D and B respectively. And finally C for the one octave part. It was so unexpected that for the first time I too laughed.

"*Chopsticks*?!" screeched Scarlett.

John handed me the spliff and I took a drag, soon followed by another.

"I believe that its official title is actually the *Celebrated Chop Waltz*," said Johnnie smiling broadly, "and as you can see," he nodded in my direction, "the ladies love it."

I laughed again and kept on laughing. Soon I could not be sure how much I had smoked only that each of the faces in front of me had started to blur into a long undulating streak of pink and brown and red and yellow, and that this horrid mass of faces was rushing towards some unknown but frightening place. For a second I considered screaming, only I was scared of going any faster.

Movies

But then everything stopped. The van pulled out in front of us and the car and then myself slowly crumpled into its rear. I was still conscious and yet my limbs, which lay like a bloody, crumpled ball of tissue, refused to answer me no matter what I said. I knew that there was someone else, a woman, lying beside me in the wreckage and that she might be able to help but before I could reach out to her I jerked awake.

I realised that I was still in Johnnie's apartment but that everything was now dark bar an illuminated rectangle—what I assumed must be the door to the bedroom—and the film that was playing on the giant television screen:

A girl in a short ill-fitting school uniform that barely contained her breasts was pleading with her English teacher not to fail her while her English teacher, a bald muscular man in a bow tie, slapped a ruler against his palm and then, despite being someone who had apparently studied Literature, said, "You want to pass so bad? I want to see just how bad you really want to pass!"

The girl bit her bottom lip, widened her eyes and nodded, then lifted up her skirt and lay down across the desk. The teacher contemplated her bare behind for a moment or so and then began to spank it with the ruler. Every time the ruler hit the girl's buttocks he asked her what else was she prepared to do. Was she prepared to go before the entire school-board for example? Yes, yes she whimpered, writhing in mock-pain and mock-ecstasy, she was prepared to do . . . *anything*. The English Teacher stopped and shook his head - but was she prepared to *really work for it . . ?*

A group of men, presumably the aforementioned school board then entered the room and formed a semi-circle around the girl who was now crouched and naked on top of the desk. The men's heads were out of shot but their dicks, each one of which the girl then tried with quiet desperation to suck, dominated the screen. Thick, spitty arcs looped from her lips to their genitals as she moved between them and sometimes, particularly when a stray hand grabbed her by the hair so that one or other of the men could force himself deeper into her she made a choking sound. The men who were not having their dicks sucked at any given moment slapped her thighs and told her to work it, or fingered her cunt . . .

Despite or because of my own persuasions I had always been a lightweight when it came to pornography—or perhaps to any physical activity filmed in high definition—and the sight of so many what I wished were private parts was one that turned my sensitive stomach. I searched for but failed to find the remote, but unearthed my phone in the process and called an Uber. As I put my phone back in my bag I saw that the school-board had now tied the schoolgirl's hand and wrists together and that the emphasis had shifted entirely to her anus.

"Yeah," said the English teacher, who still did not appear to be any more articulate, "Yeah that's right. Open her up."

Sound Waves

It was four AM when I finally reached home. My mouth was still dry with the sweet ashy taste. My brain was still addled. And the scent of sandalwood soap that permeated the pair of men's pyjamas still folded under one of the pillows provided me with yet another distraction from the unpredictability of sleep. Eventually I reached for my phone and called Albion's number, reminding myself to swop the naught for a plus-four-four. Then I did so again. And again. Ten times in all and each time just to hear it go to voicemail, meaning each time just to listen to his voice.

It was the same smooth professional voice that he had used to win over the rich old women at the charity dinner. It was also the voice that he used—or used to use - with me in public and in bed. Waiters, taxi-drivers, old school friends, and so on were sometimes privy to a warmer, softer way of speaking; a sign that he no longer felt the need to hide behind the veneer that his position in life or vision of himself more usually required. I of course had always preferred his professional voice because I never wanted him to cease trying to impress me . . .

I put down the phone and went into the bathroom. On my dentist's recommendation I had switched to an electric brush but having not yet grown used to the sensation I often laughed as it tickled my gums. I pressed 'on' and sure enough a series of involuntary gasps rose over the buzzing. I turned the toothbrush off. My phone started ringing. I went back into the bedroom and saw Albion's name on the screen. I let it go to voicemail then listened to his message:

"Allegra, hi, I'm awake now. Please call back. I miss you."

He sounded sleepy. I listened again. He sounded sleepy. But also as though he might have been talking to a waiter, taxi-driver, or old school friend. I deleted the message then changed the settings to remove the voicemail option. I went into the living area and looked at my Montagnana guarding the door to Albion's study. I wondered whether or not I would ever have sex again or want to. I was crying as well as laughing. My gums still tickled. I went back into the bathroom and rinsed my mouth with mouthwash. I didn't know whether or not I was still stoned.

Earthed

I tried again to sleep but couldn't and after an hour or more of tossing and turning in the darkness I got up again and bundled my swimming things into a bag. As I walked out into the cold, grey dawn it occurred to me that this type of light or scene could only belong to this country at this moment now. I headed up the hill to the newsagents and watched as the deliveries arrived. Piles of papers were stacked on the pavement. Most had been printed in red, white, and blue text so as to coordinate with the photographs of the men who would have been gammon-pink had they painted their faces with Union Jacks. 'Forgotten People Regain Control' said The Mail, 'Changed Forever' said The Express, and 'We are not independent. We are simply isolated' on the cover of the Guardian.

I went inside. On the left of the till was a display of shortbread biscuits all of which depicted the Royal Family: the Queen in a square hat and coat both realised in the same bright colour, Prince William and Kate Middleton dressed as a middle-aged couple, Prince Harry looking like a young James Hewitt . . . I examined the selection of chocolate bars and felt a sudden craving for Snickers but purchased a can of coke instead. I drank it immediately then immediately purchased a packet of chewing gum and put three pieces of it in my mouth in an attempt to get rid of the taste. I noticed that one of the biscuit tins had been decorated with a border of golden corgis and that Prince Harry's pupils were red. As I exited my neighbour, Helena Bonham-Carter, entered. We smiled and waved politely at each other.

Pond Life

I carried on walking towards the Heath, then through the Heath until I reached the Ladies' Pond. I paid the voluntary fee and entered the changing rooms. The air was damp against my skin and this together with the lighting lent the scene the same greenish tint as verdaccio underpainting would have done.

I took off my clothes and reached for my swimming-costume and as the heavy stretchy fabric restrained my breasts I thought once again of the Consultant - because I needed to think of someone but couldn't bear to dwell on Albion anymore. I was sure that my first memory if it was a true one had been of being swaddled and if it was false then my first fantasy —perhaps an altogether stronger thing—was of this image also. Throughout my adolescence there had been no one to care for me besides my incompetent parents, frustrated and mediocre musicians who had only ever been able to relate to me as the artist that they themselves had hoped to be and not the child that I at that time was. Left to my own meagre devices I had resorted to pricking my thighs with pins, rationing my food, and other ill-advised attempts to control my disobedient flesh through daily tests to see what it could bear, and just as I had gradually grown used to these bodily manifestations of my inferiority then, the aura of unwellness that I now excluded had likewise all too soon come to define me. Yet the changing room's greenish light together with the outdated looking wrist-support heightened these feelings to such an extent that they now became all consuming. Suddenly I was desperate to escape my current feminine confines and abandoning my clothes, which were still lying in a crumpled, costly heap, I made a dash towards the water.

Snake

The lifeguard was not in her chair, but talking to an agitated group of women who had gathered beneath the trees. Their expressions, which ranged from horror to dismay, were focused on the ground in front of them. My first thought was of a fallen nest filled with smashed eggs or baby birds' corpses but then I wondered if it was something more unsavoury, possibly involving used condoms and syringes.

"I suppose it must have escaped," said a woman to the lifeguard's right.

"I suppose the cold must have killed it," said another.

"Well, either way it's a good thing that it's dead," said the lifeguard and poked a stick at whatever it was that was lying in the grasses, "You wouldn't want that coming up behind you, now would you?"

I moved closer and saw what they did: a python of at least six or even seven feet in length lay stretched out by their feet. It was filled with maggots that made the snakeskin sides pulse and ripple. I got down on my hands and knees in order to look more closely and then immediately wished I hadn't. The stench was putrid. I gagged, put my hand over my mouth and still on all fours turned around, the dry grasses scratching against my shins as I did so. I could see that a man and a woman's name had been carved into the trunk of one of the trees and underneath the word, 'forever'. I vomited. Then stood up and before any of the other women could offer to help me ran back to the pond.

Normally I would have tried to distract myself in the same way that I always tried to distract myself now that razor blades and fasting were, I hoped, behind me, which was by thinking about the pieces that I would practice once I was home. Before the accident my morning swim had provided a moment of calm during which I would mentally list the scales and then the solo parts I planned to work on, oblivious to anything besides their names and the soft, cool pressure of the water, but now that this was no longer a possibility I tried to focus on how best to occupy myself until the evening and the concert that I had somewhat reluctantly said I would attend. I considered walking up to Highgate Cemetery but knew that the beautiful stone statues with flowers piled up around them were guaranteed to make me jealous. I considered walking up to Kenwood House but I associated oil paint with my husband which led me back to the rotting phallus in the grasses. I considered playing dead, pricking my thighs with pins, and rationing my food, which like everything else led nowhere-

"Perhaps it was someone's pet," came the lifeguard's voice from behind me, "in a strange way it's pretty."

Etudes Boreales

Eventually I opted to walk to the concert which, being in The City, used up much of my preceding time. Journalists, composers, conductors, as well as numerous musicians whom I had once been accompanied by were already in the audience. I made sure to keep my head down and took my seat as soon as I arrived and yet once the lights dimmed and the curtain lifted the situation because even worse.

I saw that she—because a man would not have been cruel enough—had the same pale oval face that I did but with the addition of Asian eyes, and thin hair scraped back in the manner of those who thought less about their appearances than their art. She was young enough to get away with it however, twenty-one at most, and yet the performance that ensued was a mature one. The way the piece allowed the girl to showcase her skill, jumping expertly to any point on the fingerboard and then beyond it, made me see it for what it was—a clever choice—despite also being one that lacked any of the sensuality for which my own work had been known. When she finished I made a show of my appreciation, slapping my good hand against the wrist-support until confident that my own performance as a 'special guest' — a title to which I would, I suspected, increasingly fall victim — was complete I swallowed bile and went in search of the bar.

Old Photographs

It was still early and the foyer was filled with natural light making the small crowd that now hurried towards the soloist appear more attractive and therefore important than was usual. I had many memories of many brilliant recitals that an occasion such as this could have prompted me to recall and yet the only one that I could think of now was, predictably, of the first time that Albion had seen me play. The concert – a typical Radio Three affair drawled through by Patrick Trelawny – had taken place at Wigmore Hall and as I flamed beneath the gold-leafed Soul of Music all of my own emotions — all of my own desperate and unceasing desire to be desired — had passed through me, into my cello, and then out into the world. For the first time I had felt complete and as if we, or I, was playing for Albion, or us, alone . . .

This auditorium was more contemporary however, albeit it equally flattering to a caucasian skin-tone and Verity whom I now joined beneath a neon sculpture that spelled out 'FEELINGS' was positively radiant with veganism. The warmth with which she greeted me once again took me back to my past but this time my past with her via an article in one of the Sunday papers. It had not only hailed me as a genius but had also been accompanied by a fashion spread in which I modelled an array of bell-sleeved gowns that despite supposedly being based on a design by William Morris showed a lot of leg. I was then still a student who had not yet completed their first year and had feared, quite rightly, that the article would provoke jealousy from my peers. Consequently I became so scared of entering the Academy on the Monday that proceeded publication that I hid in the alleyway beside it gnawing at the dead skin around my nails until I was almost down to the bone. It was Verity—warm, innocent Verity—who had come to find me of course, and so been the first to hear my lies; my feigned disgust at the interviewer's 'exaggerated claims' and even more so the fashion spread, which I denounced as 'mainstream piffle' even though it had in part been my idea ...

Ivan the-

I shook myself back into the present. In the distance I could also see Ivan—or Ivan the Terrible as we his former protégées had liked to call him—purposefully, provocatively flouting the smoking ban with one of his foul smelling Polish cigarettes. He caught my eye and began to head toward me, spilling a little from each of the drinks that were clutched against his chest as he went along. Much to my surprise he embraced Verity

first, smiling as he did so, so that to the casual observer it would have appeared as if she and not I had once been his star pupil even though having once been his star pupil I had seldom if ever made him smile.

"You seem well?" he said, still clutching and splashing the drinks, "Very healthy, yes?"

"Oh yes. I'm feeling much better thank you," said Verity.

"Soon you will be as strong as an ox again!"

I suppressed the urge to laugh at the thought of Verity's tiny, fragile figure blown up to ox-like proportions while at the same time feeling annoyed that my own health or lack of it had not been commented on. Meanwhile Ivan put down the glasses that by this point had very little liquid in them and then finally turned towards me.

"So? What did you make of my new discovery?"

"I . . ." and then, "Modest," in my firmest but also breeziest voice, "as well as mature."

"Yes. Precisely. But she needs to let herself *feel*. You know, that was always what set you apart Allegra, the depth of your *feelings*."

He raised his hand and pointed gleefully, not at the FEELINGS sculpture but at the 'No Smoking' sign that was also hanging over us and then at a flyer lying on one of the nearby tables. A map of Europe in which England had been substituted by a treble clef covered the front and it was on this section specifically that he now proceeded to flick his cigarette, until the whole of it was covered in ash and Verity started coughing.

"Oh look, I think that's Hale," she said while at the same time pointing at the clumsy, pointless figure out the window. "Now Allegra, please," and as she moved away she pressed a crumpled package into my arms, "Listen to your body."

"But . . ."

But already she was gone. Ivan and I watched her little figure retreating and for a moment there was silence.

I felt too ill to care whether or not it was uncomfortable but after a while Ivan said, "So what will you do now?"

"I . . ." I felt the prickles moving slowly through my hand, then up through my arm, and then settling in the base of my spine. "I . . ." I tried again and then, "I'm not sure I have the stamina to do anything else. Or to be anything else."

"Or the stomach?"

"Yes. That's right. I have a very sensitive stomach."

I looked past him. Through the glass and towards Hale who was now helping Verity into his stupid car. Then watched as it spluttered off into the distance revealing my younger Asian self wrestling with her cello behind it.

Ivan followed my gaze and said, "Still covered in graffiti."

"But she looks so prim and proper."

He laughed, but not quite kindly.

"I'm talking about my car.   After the referendum. 'Go Home Scum' on the bonnet."

"Oh I *see*," and then, afraid that just like our mentor-mentee days he would now turn against me on account of this, one wrong note, "England disgusts me."

"Yes, but it is still *you*," by which I assumed he meant you English, "who should be pitied." He brushed the ash from the flyer then waved it in front of my face. "But as you know Allegra, I am not the type to hold a grudge - and that is why I'm going to put you forward for *Music Without Borders*. Hui Yin," and I realised that this must be his protégée's name, "dropped out when she discovered that she was up for *Young Artist of the Year* – which means that there is still a possibility that you could join *my*" and the pleasure he gleaned for the possessive article was all to obvious "entourage for a little British Council funded escapade."

"I . . ." I began, equally repulsed by the thought of remaining in England and of leaving it in a, professionally, subordinate position. "I . . ."

"You?"

"Me. Me, myself, and I."

This time we both laughed as though back in tune with one another.

"*You*," said Ivan, "are going to come with *me*, to Athens-"

"Athens?"

"Yes Allegra, Athens. It will be good for you because . . ."

Because it was Athens. Already I had stopped listening, and lost myself in all the other thoughts that this one word provoked. *Athens* . . . And I breathed in his once disgusting now rosemary scented smoke. *Athens, Athens, Athens*, and then, *Albion! Albion! Albion!* And each time I no longer tasted ash or vomit but salt. And each time I no longer saw our cold, flat future in the Netherlands but our soft, warm past in Greece . . . I was aware of Ivan fingers toying with a small gold lighter and then thought of the Aegean sun burning even brighter than my hair . . .

"Athens is where I spent my honeymoon," I said finally.

FEELINGS

As soon as I reached home I changed into a pair of flannelette pyjamas and ripped open Verity's gift; a herbal concoction called Sleepytime Tea. The picture on the front of the packet—a bear who was also in pyjamas and snoozing by a fire—was strangely comforting. In spite of my reservations I made a cup, arranged myself on the sofa and under the Montagnana's watchful eye opened my laptop. I had one new email, clicked on it and read:

Hey,

Is your phone playing up? I keep trying to call, but for some reason don't seem able to leave a message. Anyway, I know you're busy, but I wish that you were here to see the bureaucratic nightmare that I have inherited. This morning I went to adjust one of the paintings and out of nowhere a gallery assistant shouted "Don't touch that! Please sitzt you . . .". Apparently I am not authorised to actually touch anything in the show even though I am curating it!

Speaking of which, when do you think that you'll be able to make it over? We have a dinner planned that might be interesting and/or embarrassing. The Dutch like to invite all the local dignitaries—the Mayor, the Ambassador etcetera—and so of course you'd feel at home (Ha! Ha!). In the meantime, if you could please send my books? I have an intern here called Anker who can help you if you'd like. Out of all the Museum staff she seems the most Anglo-Saxon – i.e. easy to deal with.

Lastly, I am missing you. Remember when we were here, together, at Christmas and you were wearing that ridiculous Puffa jacket? Today it would be only summer dresses. I want that right now.

Albion X

I stared at the email for a long, long time. The line about the books stood out. Because the books were a heavy and difficult thing to move, meaning that moving them to Amsterdam signified moving to Amsterdam permanently. 'If you could please send my books . . .'. If you could please stop faffing about. If you could please make one small but significant and therefore permanent gesture befitting to a wife . . . And yet significance, permanence were heavy things to come to terms with. Significant changes. Permanent losses. Significant changes to permanent losses. Permanent changes to significant losses . . . And because I now lacked anything of any significance or possessed anything that anyone of any significance would want to possess, even temporarily, I suffered from a significant, permanent lack . . .

And this lack of reason kept on spiralling until I became a dumb animal chasing its own tail. My head as well as my stomach began to ache with it. I began to fear throwing-up a second time that day. I closed my email, closed my eyes, and then almost as if I were consulting the I Ching typed 'dating websites' into google. The ache eased slightly. I opened my eyes and desperate for the lightest form of escape—or escapism from my idea of my husband and thus myself—I clicked on the first link that then appeared. A create-profile-box immediately followed and I clicked on it also, and then another box that said, *First upload some photographs* popped up.

Although I knew better than to think that fame in the world of classical music constituted fame per se my promotional photographs seemed too . . . promotional. Yet, bar a jpeg of a random Pre-Raphaelite stunner or a beautiful stone statue wreathed in flowers what other options were there? I took a deep breath and then a sip of Sleepytime tea and opened the *XMAS2015* folder. Inside were pictures of frozen canals, a gingerbread house, and myself in the aforementioned Puffa jacket. I took another sip and opened *Analogue-Fog*. After much deliberation I selected three recent scans of old photographs. The first had been taken shortly after Albion and I had started seeing each other on an occasion which, still wanting to appear at all times affable, I had been persuaded to hold a puppy. I concluded that the second must have been taken shortly after one of my New York performances due to the long, emerald dress that I was wearing. The third was from our honeymoon. In Athens.

I took another deep breath and another sip of tea and uploaded each picture. Then as an afterthought I adjusted my age to match them. A new box that said, *Introduce yourself appeared.* I typed, *Hello, pleased to meet you, I'm Allegra* and then, after a minute or so,

Looking for someone fun, a fan of music, art and travel.
Then changed it to, *Looking for someone fun looking for some fun.* And then, *Looking for someone prepared to sacrifice* their *dignity for* my *vanity.* I took another sip of tea a little of which dribbled down the front of my pyjamas. I thought about whether or not I wanted to be the bear or simply be beside him but that either way it had looked very warm and cosy in his cottage. Then took another breath and another sip, dribbled a bit more and typed:

> *Hello, pleased to meet you, I'm Allemande. I do not like to talk about my feelings although I have never shrunk from the physical expression of them; a statement that can be applied in relation to what was once the success of what was once my career or to 'having fun' when used as a euphemism for having sex although, being a (late) Romantic (and in particular a Rachmaninoff aficionado) it was most usually my former partner that I took it out on. Besides the above I regularly partake in cultural activities, socialising with the rich and would be richer (after which, on one occasion, I witnessed an Arthur de Lulli recital on a black lacquered baby grand) as well as attending art exhibitions and openings. Although these latter behaviours stem, primarily, from a sense of duty*

as opposed to quest for pleasure—real or
anticipated—something deep within me, some
form of intrinsic masochism perhaps, means
that through the act of being literally present at
these events, or alternatively of being seen at
them, I feel validated. It is almost as if the act
of being there/being seen is the only way I have
to prove, or even believe in, the value of my own
existence and hence I have now come to regard
the act of being observed in a particular place,
and being 'in the moment' as being
interchangeable phenomena. Speaking of which
what is your strangest internet experience? I
sincerely hope that this is already mine . . .

Essentialism

I fell asleep on the sofa then woke to dead devices. Again I went swimming and came back to empty, stretching hours that were no longer filled with cello practice or selecting expensive clothing. I hung my costume over the cold summer radiator and wandered aimlessly from the bedroom to the bathroom to the kitchen before finally picking up the envelope that was lying on the doormat.

I looked at the Montagnana and said, "Well, well, well, what have we got here then?"

In response, silence. I waited and then when I was sure that nothing else was going to come went and stood behind it and, turning my back on Albion's study, wrapped my arms around its shoulders. I rocked it gently back and forth cooing and crooning but nothing. I hugged it tighter still. I stroked its neck. I let my good hand pluck the strings that made a hollow sound.

In a light, playful voice I said, "Not in the mood?" and then in a serious one, "Don't worry, I'll get it back. I promise."

I let go and returned to the envelope. I picked up a butter knife and made a slit along the top and the latest series of promotional photographs slithered out onto the floor. Each one depicted my face—all the lines on which had been replaced with a uniform, digitally enhanced glow—with the album's title, *The Essential Le Clef,* emblazoned across the bottom.

"This one?" and I held up a picture in which my head was a little to the right, "Or this one?" followed by one in which it was a little to the left and then more to myself than my Montagnana, which still continued to ignore me, "Yes, yes, I know. Much of a muchness really . . ."

Vangelis

I sat down, plugged in my phone, and called the number that Ivan had given me.

It rang twice and then, "Hello, British Council. Laura speaking."

"Hello Laura, this is Allegra Le Clef."

"Alvera La . . ?"

"Allegra Le Clef. I've been asked to take part in *Music Without Borders*. In Athens-"

"A dance class? Is it in Ioannina?"

"No, a err, a musical initiative. In Athens. I'm a cellist. I'm-"

"Putting you through to the Arts Office. Please hold."

The theme from *Chariots of Fire* surged into my ear. Whenever I heard a film score I thought of Verity and other less successful contemporaries of mine who topped up their salaries with these 'gigs'. Obviously I myself had never had to stoop below the concert hall and although I had sometimes wondered what it would be like to work within the relatively more youthful milieu of synth and strings ultimately I preferred Bach, and I was happy to play Bach, essentially, forever. Because I had liked being what, until recently, had essentially been me-

"Hello, British Council Arts Office. Katie speaking."

"Hello Katie, this is Allegra Le Clef."

"And how can I help you Ms Le Clef?"

"Well, my mentor- I mean my colleague, Ivan the- Ivan, well he's been in touch about a musical-"

"Putting you through to *Music Without Borders*. Please hold."

Chariots of Fire rose again and fell again and rose again, the tinkling piano in tune with the promotional photographs' static yet luminous flicker. I pictured myself running in slow motion along endless existential beaches. I pictured myself running forward and running forward but always taking two steps back-

"Hello, British Council Arts Office. *Music Without Borders*. Lucy speaking."

"Hello Lucy, this is Allegra Le Clef."

"*The* Allegra Le Clef?"

I looked at the Montagnana, stuck my middle finger up and said, "Fuck you."

"I'm sorry? Ms Le Clef? You seem to be breaking up, you seem-"

"The reception is bad. I'll go nearer to the window." I tapped my feet on the floor, letting them rise and fall in the same slow motion as the music but without ever leaving my chair. "Ah, yes that's better."

"Oh yes Ms . . . Ms Le Clef. What I mean to say is what an honour. Mr Kamiński mentioned that you might be interested but-"

"But it sounds like a fascinating project. And I'm very fond of Greece."

"Oh that's just fantastic. To have someone of your reputation. Someone so . . ."

I looked at the Montagnana, jerked my good hand back and forwards and mouthed 'wanker'.

"So essential?"

"Yes exactly. I mean, I could arrange a lunch date for one of our representatives to fill you in. There's a very nice Greek restaurant quite near to our offices. But only if you have time. I- I mean we-"

"I have time."

Eros

Two days later I put on my most flattering dress and took a taxi to the restaurant that Katie had suggested. The Georgian brickwork had been covered in a thick, purposefully crumbling plaster and then white washed, with paintings of classical ruins realised in a dull terracotta hung across them, thus creating an effect that wasn't so much Greek as a lifestyle magazine's version of it-

"Ms Le Clef?"

"Allegra, please."

"Allegra," and the baritone dropped even deeper as it swallowed a mouthful of food, "I am Eros, and may I say on behalf of everyone at the British Council that we are happy as the clams that you will soon be visiting us. It will be a great feather in our cap as you say."

I sat down trying not to laugh either at his quaint mishmash of idioms or his eating habits which, together with his long sallow face and his long lashed mournful eyes, made me think of a donkey with its head half buried in a nosebag. The fact that he had already started eating told me both that he was a general arts representative as opposed to a specific music one—or he would have been far too intimidated to take such a liberty—as well as his being either new to or not much caring for his job. Under normal circumstances I would have felt insulted by his behaviour but nothing about my circumstances was normal anymore and his very lack of ceremony, I was surprised to realise, was what actually made me feel at ease.

Without meaning to I said, "I was in Athens—a while ago now—but I can still remember how it smelled. The pine trees. And also orange blossom."

I waited as Eros extracted a lettuce leaf from one of the many salads that were already in front of him and then with great pathos began to tear it into pieces.

He looked up briefly from his plate and said, "It was a happy time?"

"Yes. Yes, it was," and now that I had finally begun to talk of Albion out loud—and to someone about whom I knew nothing, and to whom I owed nothing, and did not appear to know anything either significant or permanent of me—I found that I couldn't stop myself from talking and in a deep rush of breath continued, "We, my lover- I mean my husband- and I, we flew in on Good Friday. The funeral bells were ringing and they kept on ringing throughout the day and into the middle of the night. At dusk we joined a procession led by monks carrying a giant crucifix – it took six of them just to lift it - and as they walked towards the cemetery they sang. It was beautiful, only as soon as we reached our destination it began to rain. My husband grabbed my hand and we ran, together, along the broken pathways and took shelter under one of the Cyprus trees. I remember that it was very black and very tall and just the same as all the others . . ."

The Waitress came over and deposited a plate of octopus stew on Eros' side of the table. I was about to ask her for a menu but before I had chance to do so she disappeared. Seemingly oblivious to everything besides his own immediate hunger Eros reached for a fork and speared a long dark tentacle.

Disgusted, I turned away and looking not at him but at the paintings I continued, "The next day we caught a boat to one of the islands. There were so many things that we wanted to do, but we were so tired that as soon as we reached our rented cottage we fell fast asleep. When we woke the air was thick with smoke that smelled of rosemary. We went outside to see what it was. A small boy walked past and gave us each an egg, dyed red with onion skins, and instructed us to bang the ends together. We did as he suggested and my egg smashed into my husband's . . ."

"And your husband will be coming with you? To Athens?"

"No," and then, "He's curating an exhibition. In Amsterdam."

"He's an artist?"

"An art historian."

Eros looked thoughtful. Then put down his fork. He typed something into his phone and handed it to me. A series of rectangles depicting a grim, industrial building situated on the side of a motorway filled the screen. I couldn't see what if anything they had to do with *Music Without Borders* but I saw the fact that he had at least temporarily stopped eating as a positive and so pulled what I hoped was an interested face.

"This is the art new gallery, or rather it was meant to be," he said eventually, "Inside there are empty bookshelves where the bookshop is meant to be, and empty chairs and tables where the cafeteria is meant to be, and huge empty rooms where the art is meant to be. But nothing that is meant to be has yet become."

He took back his phone, and typed something else into it. Then offered it to me again. This time the rectangles were filled with giant space age blocks joined together by a solar panelled canopy.

"And this is the Cultural Centre where classical musicians play. It was built with private money from private sponsors, and is designed to tell a story, namely that Greece is still a civilising force, and also to remind us, the civilised world, that this is the world that Greece gave birth to."

"Oh . . . ?" and then still trying to understand, "And are you an artist Eros?"

"Yes. Yes, I am." A flush of pleasure crept up his neck so deep and pink that would have thought that like his namesake he had feasted not on octopus but roses, "Actually Ms- Allegra. Ever since you walked in I have very much been wanting to ask you something. Allegra, please, when we have had our just desserts, you would like to come up and- and see my etchings as you say?"

Suite No. 3, Op. 87

I waited somewhat impatiently while Eros paid the bill and then we set off towards his studio. Throughout the journey we continued to make polite conversation and to behave as if his previous proposal and my tacit acceptance of it had not occurred. Every so often the image of a long dark tentacle moving between his lips would resurface but each time I pushed it down again. I thought that it would do me good to feel the weight of all those dinners on top of me and to prove to myself that even without my husband and with my injuries I was still not entirely sexless and therefore still retained some small value in the world.

A few more minutes of small talk and we reached what appeared to be a boarded-up block of apartments. Eros unlocked a metal door and led the way up a flight of metal steps. Then he stopped and unlocked another door that this time had a heavy chain stretched across it. Inside was a large square room empty but for a very cheap stereo, plan-chest, printing-press and a much stained futon that I now sat down on.

There were pots of ink and rags piled up in one corner and a series of scratched copper squares leaned against the damp, concrete walls.

"Now I will set the mood," said Eros.

He flicked a switch and Britten began to play. For a moment I was transported, away from the grimy studio and into the heart of the suite. Again I tasted salt but now it was accompanied by the scent of incense, of orthodox churches and funerals and cemeteries as well as sparkling water. Again I recalled what had until recently been the type of past that suited the type of someone I had been. The memory of Albion that was the memory of us. The memory of us that was the memory of England, and of Athens. The memory of England and of Athens that was the memory of Europe, of unity, of a beautiful dream that had failed . . .

"Another thing that I remember was the sea," I said kicking off my shoes and leaning back against the dirty futon, "after we had eaten our eggs we went swimming. My costume was green and my husband- I mean my lover- Well he joked that I was a mermaid. I laughed and said that if he wasn't careful I would swim away. So he grabbed hold of me and bit my shoulder - so hard that he drew blood and his teeth left a scar in the shape of a circle . . ."

I paused as Eros sat down on the floor in front of me, which brought his face to the same level as my thighs. This time I forgot the tentacles but remembered the nosebag. Again I pushed it down and then moved my legs so that they were very slightly apart. Eros leaned forward. Then reached towards the bottom drawer of the plan-chest and slowly pulled it open. He removed a sheaf of papers and very carefully began to lay them out around my feet. Each one varied in size as well as technique, some utilising the hard controlled lines of dry-point and others the woozier ones of soft-ground etching. Yet the subject matter was always the same: Athens at dusk and the impenetrable Cyprus trees rising in black, phallic spears around the edges of the paper. I looked at them and looked at them and then finally understanding I laughed – and just as loudly as I would have done had he been playing *Chopsticks*.

Jerusalem

Once home I threw the pile of unwanted etchings that Eros had insisted I take with me on top of the unwanted promotional photographs and then went straight for the laptop. My inbox was full of messages sent via the dating website all of which were awful. Fat old men whose wives didn't understand them, gym-toned twenty-two year olds looking for experiences via pictures of their naked chests, and a basset hound underneath which the 'owner' went into some detail regarding his erotic obsession not with dogs but human feet. I deleted all of them, clicked 'compose' and then in one long stream of not-quite-consciousness typed the following:

Dear Albion,

Sorry not to have been in touch sooner, but everything here has been so hectic. The record company are still vamping up the Essential Le Clef *even though, as I keep on telling them, all that Sexiest Classical Musician stuff just isn't necessary. The Greatest Classical Musician of the Century would be more appropriate, or even The Greatest Classical Musician. Plus, the British Council have been in touch about a new initiative, which they're hoping I'll spearhead for them - in Athens! Of course this means that I might arrive in Amsterdam a little later than expected, but how can I say no? The Greeks feel as though the rest of the world has forgotten them—probably because, besides cut-price holidays in Mykonos, the rest of the world has —and while I hate to sound vain, having someone with my reputation endorse the program really will make a difference. And as you know I really *do* care.*

All my love, my love

Allegra X

Straight away I pressed send, knowing that had I read back through it then my lies by omission (namely my failure to mention either the Consultant or his advice as well as all the reasons as to why I had been unable to pick up my phone) would have jumped out at me; just as my lies by lying (namely that it was not I alone who had been asked to visit Athens or indeed to lead the Athens visit) would have come back to haunt me later on. I also suspected that, even in my very worst, worst moments I would have balked from the 'The Greatest Classical Musician of the Century' but the strain of sending the email or alternatively the strain of trying to act natural was already so great that the thought of having to formulate my deceits into anything more than the cartoon-awfulness was overwhelming . . .

I closed my email and closed the laptop. Then re-opened the laptop and re-opened *Analogue-Fog* but this time I clicked on the pictures of my honeymoon only; a point in time before I had had chance to appear as my most awful, all-consuming self. I saw that most of the now bigger and blurrier rectangles were still of me—either squinting into the bright spring sunshine or else through the dark of an orthodox shrine—while what small pieces of Albion were visible most usually took the form of his thumb over the lens. I looked and looked at his thumb but the meaning of it escaped me.

Arrangements

Again I went to bed again, woke up again, went swimming again and then came home to a home that wasn't my home anymore. Again. I stepped over the pool of images beside the coffee table. Again it was early in the empty and endless day. I looked at the Montagnana and then my phone and then my laptop.

Then looked at the Montagnana again and said, "Yes, yes. I know."

I prodded the wrist-support. It was still slightly soggy from the Pond. The water had made dark patches on what had until now been a dull, sticking plaster pink so that in places it resembled a portwine stain. One of the straps had come loose and dangled at the bottom end in the same way that I imagined the fastenings on a straightjacket would have done had they been to scale. Unless of course it was a child's straightjacket. And then did children have straightjackets? And then . . .

I looked at the Montagnana and said, "You know if you're not careful my body will run away with me."

Then gritted my teeth and did up the strap, pulling it so tightly that it hurt. Then resumed staring at the laptop. I was just about to give in and log-on to the dating website when my phone started ringing. It was an unknown number but I still picked up.

"Yes?" I said curtly,

"Hello, Ms Le Clef?"

"Speaking."

"Hello Ms Le Clef, this is Hayley. I'm calling about your operation . . ."

It could have been a doll's straightjacket I thought suddenly. Or a teddy-bear's. It could have been a prop in a sinister children's game which, having been a serious and solitary child, was what most children's games had always seemed to me to be. I saw my smaller, lesser self waiting for one of the bigger, better kids to choose me. I saw myself lingering on the sides then running home to practice, practice, practice, starve and snip . . .

". . . So shall we say Tuesday?"

I looked at the Montagnana but it remained imperious. I looked at the wrist-support and then the laptop.

"Ms Le Clef?"

I made a V sign at the Montagnana and said, "See. You. Next. Tuesday."

"Fantastic. That's all booked. And if you've got any questions then please, don't hesitate to call."

She hung up and I sat in silence like a lover or a loveless child who was always waiting. And then I called Scarlett who because she was in love gave no reply. But I remained where I was on the sofa willing the phone to ring. And then the phone rang.

"Yes?" I said, curtly. Again.

"Allegra?" came Verity's breathless reply.

"No."

"Oh yes, ha ha. And the operation? Do you have a date?"

"Next Tuesday."

"I see. And Athens?"

"The day after."

"But won't that be-"

"No."

And even though it was lightness, even sympathy, that I had wanted my thoughts became as dark and solid as my cello, my husband, or a cemetery filled with Cyprus trees. Plus the Montagnana who had finally caught my eye was smirking. I could hear Hale making unnecessary noises in the background. I thought of his stinking car and all the other stupid reasons why he refused to be sorry and ashamed. I thought of Verity's rainbow socks, which she had probably bought because they came in a multi-pack just as her underwear probably came in a multi-pack too. I thought about the 'musical shower' that filled her flute and all the other stupid, mixed-up things that filled her stupid, infantile brain including her kindness and her kindness to me in particular, and then how unfair her perfect health was-

"Well, if you're sure. Actually, there's something I've been meaning to talk to you about-" she began a little uncertainly.

"I'm sorry Verity, but can we do this another time? Something's just come up."

"Oh yes, okay, it's just . . ."

"Yes?"

"Oh don't worry. It's nothing."

Shroud

A few days later Scarlett re-emerged to drag me in and out the changing rooms of upper-end department stores. Whereas in a happier world Verity might have been my family Scarlett always made me feel like the teenage friend that as a teenager I had always longed to have.

I watched as she looked in the mirror, tugged at the ruffles on her Bardot-top and said, "But do you think that Johnnie will like it?"

"But you don't even know where you're going yet. You might not even need beachwear."

"Oh Allegra. Please."

I removed a grey silk wrap from one of the hangers and draped it over my face.

"You might need a veil."

"I might need a passport."

"You don't have a passport?"

"Yes, I have a passport, but then I thought that in light of the current political situation it might be wise to embrace my Irish roots, which means that-"

"You're a beast of no nation?"

"Ha ha."

I could see through the gauze how her nipples, once she removed the Bardot-top, stared defiantly at me as well as how, once they had made her point she quickly scooped them back into her bra. I let the wrap fall onto the floor then immediately picked it up again. Ideally I would have liked to keep it over my face until the doctors' dirty work was done. I couldn't see how a burka was any more oppressive than Scarlett's blouse was; or how a different man could cut up your face, your breasts, your labia 'just for you'; or why anyone would learn to play any instrument, would succumb to endless hours of practice, practice, practice, snipping and suffering without an audience to hear and know and prove that you and you above all others were the best . . .

I returned the wrap to its hanger and followed Scarlett back out into the store. I had intended to make a purchase purely for the sake of it and then head straight to the tearoom only before I could do so Scarlett stopped to examine one of the displays. A pyramid of soaps wrapped in oatmeal paper were heaped on the stand closest to us and an accompanying text decorated with dried grasses alluded to 'wellness' 'mindfullness' and other new age nouns.

She picked out an especially worthy looking bundle and looking at me said, "Should we get one for Verity?"

"Fuck Verity!"

"Oh Allegra, please!"

I knew that my response petty and that Verity, who in a parallel life was my sister, would no doubt like the relatively inexpensive soap, and yet I could't stop my present awful self from being awful, "Ideally, one should never give a brown present," I continued then took the bundle out of Scarlett's hands and returned it to the stand. "Plus, I think that everyone should stop indulging her. It only encourages her morbidity. Which is profound."

The Rococo Variations

I checked my messages. I had one new email via the dating website from someone called The_Saracens_79. I looked at his profile picture, which had the same dark and heavy features as the Consultant or my husband, and then at the *Introduce Yourself* box which stated:

> *As the user-name suggests I do like to watch and play rugby, but I'm also an avid reader (political thrillers) and cinema goer (mainly action movies). Although I spend most of my time working as a corporate lawyer (but don't worry, we can tell your mother that I'm the barman in a brothel!). I'm also a fairly gregarious, as well as ambitious, kinda guy . . .*

I considered the picture and the introduction as they stood. Certainly his looks were to my taste, his grammar, despite the somewhat excessive use of parentheses, conformed to the norms of the establishment and his interests and occupations were delightfully far from my own. I tapped onto his message and read:

Okay Allemande, so here goes . . .

My weirdest internet experience is quite easy to recall. In 1999 I used to frequent chatrooms on Yahoo, a then new way to connect with people from all over the world. Anyway, I got speaking with this woman (Chelsea) and we got along really well, often chatting for several hours each afternoon.

A few weeks later I got back from a long day drafting contracts (no change there!) picked up the mail and noticed an envelope with an airmail sticker on it. I opened it and it was a handwritten letter from Chelsea. My initial reaction was to freak out because I had not given her either my surname or address, and to this day I do not know how she got that information unless she hacked my computer.

The letter was extremely long, full of ridiculous over-emotional prose with her proclaiming love for me . . . in a crazy way! I logged online and left her a message questioning how she got my address and how on earth she could feel as if she was in love with me after just a few weeks messaging. She reacted defensively, but was also apologetic, saying it was a bit of a joke, but then admitting later that it wasn't . . .

I told her I didn't want any more contact and that precipitated a few weeks of actual stalking. She would follow me from chatroom to chatroom and bombard me with messages. It wasn't fun. In the end I threatened to contact the authorities and she backed off. She tried contacting me under different names, but it was easy to see through her disguises . . .

Tchaikovsky was playing in the background and this particular recording, which was of the London Philharmonic Orchestra and myself, was widely and rightfully considered to be the best one. I shut my eyes and listened as the prim beginning gave way to a luscious, full-blown abandon then opened them and took another look at my phone. Firstly he, The_Saracens_79, would have been a teenager in 1999. Secondly even teenagers studying law did not draft legal contracts. Thirdly why had he been 'speaking' with

Chelsea for several hours each afternoon if he wasn't looking for or even by default having an online relationship . . . ?

I glanced furtively behind me but Scarlett was still nowhere to be seen. I could tell from the little green circle beside The_Saracens_79's name that he was now online, which struck me as an incredibly intimate piece of information for the simple reason that unlike the others it must be true. I sent a brief message asking what had happened to Chelsea and a few more what I assumed must be flirtations pinged back and forth between us. He referred several times to his job's 'international aspects' and in response I made the obligatory Brexit jokes. A few minutes passed and another, longer message appeared:

> . . . But the referendum was, predominantly, a reaction to virtually unlimited immigration. Immigration that has changed the faces of many towns up and down the country regardless of the fact that a lot of places weren't ready, culturally or otherwise, to take on such large influxes of non-English speaking peoples.
>
> Whether the liberal-left want to admit it or not immigration does cause all sorts of problems, not least with schools, doctors' surgeries, and so on. Likewise, pockets of isolated communities that speak little to no English, and

don't seem overly interested in integration are going to have a detrimental effect on the native inhabitants of certain areas, and to label those who raise their more than understandable concerns about these matters as racist is grossly unfair in my opinion . . .

Prelude

I looked up to see Scarlett, who was holding a plate of miniature eclairs, and pleased to note that she had now resumed her more usual behaviours I smiled warmly at her.

She sat down opposite me and said, "The crazy thing is it's only been a few weeks. But it just feels so . . . *right*," then put a whole miniature eclair in her mouth, "Although if I'm honest I do wish that he'd decide on somewhere soon though. I mean if it's Italy I'd shop for things that were a bit more dressy, whereas if it's the south of France . . . All things considered though, Dublin could also be an option . . ."

She cut one of the other miniature eclairs into quarters and placed it in front of me before moving onto Johnnie's not particularly exciting sexual preferences. I was surprised that they were still together but also tired to be pleased that unlike me she seemed happy. I added nodding to the smiling followed by a series of 'umm,' 'ohh,' and 'err's while also attempting to work my way very slowly through one of the choux-pastry sections - but inwardly I was still searching for clues about The_Saracens_79. Gradually the internet merged with Eros, the Axis Occupation, and my fictitious oppression by it until I was faint with thoughts of my own, dazzling annihilation—or alternatively, all I knew of sex—and then I wondered whether I had it in me to become the new Chelsea. I too had hours of free time in which to write to my new virtual acquaintance, only our correspondence would flourish because unlike my predecessor I didn't really want to meet. Plus there was the added bonus that so long as it remained online I wouldn't technically be cheating-

"Once when my husb- I mean when Albion and I were in Athens we walked up to the top of Lycabettus Hill," I said, and as I spoke a note of urgency entered my voice. "We could see the whole city, literally glittering in front of us. The nearest beach was very dirty but we caught a bus just a little further out and the sea became a beautiful crystalline blue. I think that you and Johnnie would like it there. In fact I was just thinking that if you wanted to join me-"

"It sounds wonderful but-"

"We wouldn't have to hang out all the time, or even most it," I cut in quickly and noticing as I did so that Scarlett had not only eaten all of the remaining miniature eclairs but also the three remaining quarters on my plate. "Just that if ever you were at a loose end then I could introduce you to the British Council people.

There's always lot of dinners and parties and so on at these things. And they're actually quite fun. We could-"

"Allegra, *please*. You're sweet. But Johnnie just wants to relax. And if we went to Athens *now*, well, we just wouldn't be able to do that would we?"

Nocturne

I kept on smiling as we said our goodbyes only now that I had decided that I hated my home I dreaded going back there. The few rooms that I chose to sit or sleep in were decorated with a mixture of both authentic and reproduction Arts & Crafts pieces juxtaposed—to use the correct curatorial term—with mid-century modern ceramics. It did not seem strange to picture each room within *World of Interiors* magazine, as in fact each one had been, and yet if anyone were to look a little closer, then it soon became apparent that each one had slipped a little.

Nothing was quite as clean as it should have been and due to my repeated attempts to erase all memories of Albion while at the same time not throwing any of them away various objects—a bottle of contact lens solution say, a half-used piece of soap—were now hidden in increasingly strange places. As soon as I entered the apartment I was confronted by one of his notebooks which, for some unknown reason, had escaped the confines of his study. Without thinking I pushed it down the back of the sofa and then kicked the coffee table so that it jolted forward and hid the coffee stain that I had left to fester on the carpet.

"When I am older . . ." I began but said no more.

When I am older I will do what I want is what I had thought when I was younger. When I am older I will be beautiful, brilliant, a famous cellist even . . . And yet already I was older and soon would be old but still to all intents and purposes a woman and therefore undistinguished in my grief-

PING! went my phone.

I ran into the bedroom, which like every other room had long since ceased to be a place of safety, and looked into the dressing-table mirror. The oval shape always made me think of myself as the wicked stepmother in *Snow White*. I looked into it and remembered not only that I had always wanted to be older but also that I had never wanted to be old because I equated being old with being alone, which I equated with my childhood and being a child in pain-

PING!

I picked up my flannelette pyjamas and hung them over the mirror. Then knelt down and pulled my travel-case out from underneath the bed. Thick lugs of dust rose up and settled on my hair. I brushed the worst of them onto the floor and opened the case. Hayley had said that I would probably be able to go home that same day but nevertheless I laid a cleanish towel inside and also a book of poetry that had been well reviewed in the weekend papers. Then my spare toothbrush, toothpaste, and various other toiletries. Then make-up and more make-up going so far as to include a Chanel lipstick which, when you twisted it, looked like a dog's penis. Then a bottle of perfume made entirely from white flowers, the key chemical components of which were also present in human shit. Then a pair of seamed stockings with lace tops and a suspender belt to match them . . .

I took a breath and threw in five pairs of ribbon-tie knickers which, like the bedroom's hand-painted silk wallpaper, were also realised in apricot, oyster and cherry-pink tones suited to my colouring. When I am older, I thought sadly, winding the ribbons between my too slim fingers, this is how my corpse will be dressed.

The Postcard

I dragged the travel-case into the living area and sat down heavily on it. For the first time I noticed that the doormat's shape and particular shade of brown were near identical to a flattened-out paper bag. I focused on it and visualising it expanding and contracting I soon began to breath more slowly. As I did so I saw that there was also something lying on the top. I took another deeper breath and stood up. Then another and made my way towards the door. Then one more as I bent down and picked up the postcard. On the front was a Pre-Raphaelite painting of a woman who like all Pre-Raphaelite women resembled me. I turned it over. There were several small typed lines that revealed the postcard's origin (Tate Britain), a foreign stamp that revealed the sender's location (Jordaan, Amsterdam), and a dense copperplate paragraph in what could only be Albion's hand. I took another even deeper breath and read:

> *Greetings from the flatlands – can you guess how I am feeling? I doubt that it would be too hard, whereas you my love are still a mystery (but then again, that's how you've always liked it). I can't wait to see the new promotional pictures, and well done on* Music Without Borders *– you must do it, of course. Please send details of your arrival as soon as you know more (and in the meantime my books?).*

> *Albion X*

I sat back down and resumed staring at the doormat. I knew just as Albion wanted me to know why he had sent the postcard; because my phone-playing-up-façade was pathetic and because his emails were too easy to ignore. There were so many ways not to be forgotten, I thought glibly, the best one of which was to keep on saying that you remembered. And yet I sometimes wished that he would forget me altogether rather than destroy what could have been a perfect memory. I turned the postcard over but although this hid his written words his other visual message was now exposed. My double or else the wicked step-mother before she became the wicked step-mother stared up at me – and all at once I was enveloped by a tenderness so great that it was pitiable.

Incidental

I put the postcard down, picked up my phone and sent a rambling message to The_Saracens_79. Then I put down my phone, picked up the etchings and began to lay them out across the floor. I arranged them the same way Eros had only I turned each one upside down so that the Cyprus trees pointed inwards.

I shut my eyes and listened to the wind that blew softly down the chimney.

"Witch . . ." said the Montagnana.

The wind ceased and I scrambled back up off the floor.

"What did you just call me?"

I waited, refusing to let it stare me down and then without warning my knees buckled. I fell to the ground and the etchings fluttered out across the carpet. But still my eyes didn't leave it, or him, or me-

"What did you just call me?" I repeated.

But again there was no answer and this time I looked away.

Down at the dark phallic arrows in the etchings and then up at the wicked step-mother propped up by the travel-case beside the door and then without knowing why, I shouted, "Satan!"

The wind rose again but more insistently. I could smell the damp through the floorboards and see the branches tapping at the window. I thought of doctors' surgeries and piss and sick and disinfectant altogether.

It rose up in me, a choking vomiting coughing until once again I screamed out, "Satan!"

The wind dropped. The branches were still. The damp moved into my bones.

But still I kept on, "Satan! Satan! Satan!

Private

An hour later I checked myself into the hospital. I had a dim recollection of a nurse testing my blood pressure and drawing a dotted line with what looked like felt-tip pen around my wrist. Then an injection. Then lying on a stretcher and the memory of crumpled metal. Suddenly everything went dark. And then just as suddenly I was in the Recovery Room.

My vision was hazy but I could see that a selection of newspapers were lying on the bedside table.

The headlines ranged from 'A Nation Divided' to 'Brexit Earthquake' to 'Goodbye' in 27 languages. I reached for the first one but still groggy from the anaesthetic succeeded only in knocking them all onto the floor. The Daily Mail fell open on a list of celebrity Remain campaigners entitled 'Angry Luvvies'. It included JK Rowling, Gary Lineker and Hugh Laurie whom I had once met at a Gershwin concert-

"And how are you feeling, Allegra?"

The lighting in the Recovery Room was dim but in the corridor it came from strip-lights so that the Consultant who was stood in the doorway that joined the two now appeared in silhouette only. He seeped in an inky mass towards me and as I looked at him I shivered.

"Are you cold, Allegra?"

I nodded and tried to focus on his face which, although I could tell from the angle of his head was also looking at the Daily Mail, remained indefinite.

I attempted a smile and said, "You're neither one thing nor the other."

"Why, is my ethnicity an issue?"

"No, no if course not." I could feel my cheeks reddening, "I only meant- I mean- it's your- your edges."

"My edges?"

"They're blurry."

The Consultant burst out laughing.

Then abruptly stopped and in a tone that was close to but not apologetic said, "Allegra, you must forgive me. For a moment I thought that . . ."

"That I was the wrong sort of angry luvvie?"

"Yes. Yes, I'm sorry."

He sat down on the bed and placed his hand against my forehead, which was hot. Then took hold of my arm and checked my pulse, which raced. I knew that the eroticism with which these small physical occurrences were on my part imbued were due to his appearance being so similar to my husband's and yet whereas the thought of Albion having to care for my broken body filled me with disgust the Consultant's attentions hardly bothered me primarily because they seemed so far away from the possibility of real life sex. As he held my wrist I pictured the blue plaque above the Harley Street newsstand. Old Allegra had wanted her husband to beat her, bind her and fuck her senseless. Whereas poor Poorly Allegra's perversions were compatible with the Consultant's, a sad fat donkey, or a man on a dating website that she had no plans to actually meet-

"And do you feel sick, Allegra?"

"No. Yes." Again I attempted to smile. "Or no more than usual."

Vocational Training

There was a pause and I said, "So what made you decide to become a doctor?"

The Consultant wrote something down on his pad. Then looked around the room for other things that he might do. There were none.

"Well . . ." he said, "I suppose because I wanted to be of service. I felt that I had a vocation," and then quickly changing tack, "but what about you Allegra? What made you take up the cello?"

"The same. Sort of. Or I felt like I couldn't do anything else."

Or that I wasn't allowed to.

I remembered being thirteen, slowly straightening out a safety pin and pulling it in a long, red line across my thigh. Then fourteen when my diet of chewed-up, spat-out meals began. Then eighteen when Ivan had taken over and my schedule had become so gruelling that I rarely had time for any other further variations of abuse. Unlike my parents' tutelage his had left no room for even the fantasy of rebellion because there had been so many equally willing, almost as gifted young people ready and waiting to replace me in the wings. Consequently I had worked hard for him, suffered hard for him, and in place of love and blood and loss the ultimate prize: recognition. And then I had turned twenty-five, the age when I first met Albion and once again handed my neuroses over . . .

"But if I'm honest I didn't want to be of service," I said trying to read what the Consultant had written about me on his pad, "But you can't really have wanted to either. Otherwise why go into private practice?"

"Well . . . Because I became cynical. And because I hardly saw my wife."

"Oh?" I made my voice as light as possible. "That must have been . . . upsetting?"

"The thing is- *Allegra*," and I felt his weight shift uncomfortably beside me, "everybody, regardless of their politics, wants their expectations to be confirmed. A banker, an ad man, an estate agent, nobody cares if they behave badly. Because we expect it. But a doctor? A doctor is expected not only to care but to care without limits and then when we discover that in reality he can only give so much . . ."

I let my good arm drop and the neck of my dressing-gown fall open.

The Consultant took a breath then continued, "My wife and I had been going through a difficult period – several rounds of IVF that culminated in a miscarriage. Of course I knew that she was unhappy and I felt guilty for always being too tired and overworked to talk about it. But I also knew that things could not go on as they were. So I booked a table at our favourite restaurant and hoped, perhaps naively, that during the course of the evening we would begin to put things right."

"And did you?" I asked, squinting at the bare skin of my forearm which, in my current, hazy state, was indistinguishable from its plaster twin.

"Yes, but not on that occasion because as I was waiting for my train home the Station Master made an announcement. He asked for a doctor to make their way to the ticket office. He stressed that it was 'a matter of urgency.' "

"And what happened then?" I asked, stroking the warm skin and then the cold plaster.

"I discovered that one of the passengers had fallen down the stairs, knocking out several teeth, some of which had then jammed in his windpipe. The Station Master had already performed the Heimlich Manoeuvre, but without any success, and the man had now stopped breathing. The only solution was an emergency tracheotomy that I performed with a kitchen knife and a straw. The man went on to make a full recovery - but of course I was late to the restaurant."

"But you're a hero."

"Well that's what my wife said, many times, because what else could she say? But to be honest I still resent the passenger for falling and the Station Master for asking for my help because the desire to make my wife, specifically, happy in whatever minor or insignificant a way eclipsed any desire to be of service. It-" but then he stopped, in the same way that he had stopped laughing earlier, "It . . ."

"Don't worry, I understand," and, although I was still not quite sure where his face began or ended, I was sure that I smiled into something meaningful, "Love exposes our badness."

Blur

Another figure, presumably one of the nurses, was now standing in the doorway and the Consultant began to ooze towards him. They huddled together for a moment blocking the outside light. Then the nurse left, shutting the door behind him and making the Recovery Room even darker than before.

Slowly the Consultant drifted back, sat down on the bed again and said, "I suppose I ought to add that both my parents were physicians."

Without intending to I laughed. Perhaps hysterically. A light pulsating feeling in the tips of my bad fingers made me think of blood. I realised that it had been some time since I had had my period and began to wonder if I was going through an early menopause. To be cursed by no longer being cursed – it seemed so very me, or the me that was me at this moment.

I decided that now was not the time to dwell on it however when there was the more immediate problem of my vision. I found that if I focused on a single flat and unmoving surface, a newspaper say, then I could just about make out what was happening on it. I reached for the one nearest to me, which also happened to be the one with the multilingual cover, and held it up in such a way that I was sure that the Consultant must see the same thing I did.

"The only foreign words I know relate to music," I said and then almost conspiratorially, "I had a very anecdotal education."

"Anecdotal?"

The Consultant smiled and momentarily emboldened I continued, "Charming, irrelevant scraps of information related to the arts. The type of thing that makes for excellent dinner party conversation but-"

"Excuse me."

The nurse was back, and this time he tapped his watch. The sound of someone else's mobile came from the corridor behind him. Then the sound of a landline ringing. Then the sound of a printer whirring. The Consultant stood up again and oozed towards him until they formed one giant inky mess.

I looked at what was either a human being or a Rawshack Test and said, "If one of you could call me a taxi?"

Allemande

Still bleary and clumsy I kicked open the door to the apartment and flung my travel-case on the floor. Out of habit I reached for my phone. I had three new messages.

One from The_Saracens_79, one from Ivan ,and one from Albion:

Hello? Hello? Hello?

Did you get my postcard, or are you just pretending not to? I can and will send others.

Oh God, so bored.

Everyone is so fucking young here, and as you know I hate canals.

Anyway, Anker—I think that you would like her —has been showing me around and last night dragged me to a nightclub.

We're going out again tonight, although not sure if I can keep up (joke).

Let me know how you are doing, please?

And seriously, if you could at least send my books I would be eternally grateful (and still) Yours

Albion X

I threw the phone across the floor, irked by the fake-lightness and fake-playfulness that had now been extended fake-casually to Anker. Other women had always been attracted to Albion who was no good at being alone and as he had a broader and more obliging sexual repertoire than I myself did could more easily choose not to be. If he was not already eating badly then it was only a matter of time before takeaways became the norm. If he was not already wearing crumpled shirts then he soon would. And if he was not already sleeping with the intern while his difficult wife ignored him . . .

I flew like an angry sleepwalker across the living area, past the Montagnana and towards the door to Albion's study. I unlocked it, even though it had never been locked in all the time that we had lived together and had only been locked by me after he had gone. The wooden furniture was as dark and heavy as the Consultant's rooms, as was the near identical office chair. Everything else though differed drastically. The walls were almost completely covered in cuttings and reproduction prints and an oil paining, a portrait of a flame haired woman cradling a lyre which, like the postcard, had an air of being 'after-Rossetti,' while both the desk and the floor was piled high with stacks of books.

I reached for the nearest one which, thanks to my cast, immediately fell over and then one by one each of the other towers toppled. Whores that looked like Scarlett and saints that looked like Verity tumbled out of them as well as numerous red headed women who used to look like me. In the past these images would have comforted me in that they adhered to and so confirmed my neatly compartmentalised worldview. Yet now they served not only as a reminder that there was an order but also that I no longer fitted into it. That I was no longer beautiful, desirable—a conformist—and therefore no longer deserving of love.

I took a deep breath and began to stamp across the floor taking care to leave as many footprints as I could across the other women's faces. I tore down the cuttings and the prints, some of which I ripped to pieces. I went over to Albion's desk, picked up the bronze paperweight and threw it as hard as I could at the wall. The sharp edge slashed into the portrait leaving a large tear gaping in the middle of what should have been the sitter's nose. Then I gave one last kick to the only tower that was standing, turned on my heel and fled.

A Tombstone Almost

I was still breathing heavily when I reached the kitchen. A bunch of daffodils—no doubt a gift from Verity—was waiting for me on the table as well as a box of pastel coloured macarons bearing Scarlett's signature. I made an effort to be calm or at least enact calm behaviours and put the kettle on before returning to the living area. Now that I was paying attention I could see that someone had hoovered it and that both the promotional photographs and the etchings had been tidied into piles. I turned the photographs over and then placed them on top of the etchings so that my face was hidden amongst the trees. Then I turned to look at the Montagnana.

I stood with both feet planted firmly apart and in my most authoritative voice said, "Stop spying on me you little shit."

But as usual, it did not reply.

I went back into the kitchen. I made a cup of Sleepytime tea, placed three lavender macarons on the saucer, and returned to the living area. I opened my laptop, logged into my emails, and clicked compose. I chewed-up and spat-out a macaron. Then chewed-up and spat-out two more. I drank my cup of tea, got up, made another cup of tea, then sat back down again. After a while, I typed, *Hello.* And then, *Hi.* And then, *Hiya!* (although that one struck me as far too camp even for a onetime sexiest classical musician). And then, *Dear Albion.* And then, *Dearest Albion* . . . And then I deleted all of the emails in my inbox and considered but resisted also hurling my laptop across the floor.

The Montagnana reminded silent but I could tell that it was laughing. I stood up and once again turned to face it.

This time however I gritted my teeth and hissed, "You little shit, I told you to stop spying on me!" but its expression didn't change. "Stop looking at me!"

I repeated, and then, "I said stop looking at me, you cunt!"

Yet still it kept on trying to punish me for all the things about myself that I too hated until all that had until now been hardened into anger and then depression caught fire and turned into an even greater and more furious rage. I took a step backwards then ran and slammed myself as hard as I could against it—so large, so dark, *a tombstone almost*—and punched it with my cast. And then I kept on. Against it, and against it, and against it. And against it until I heard the car door crumpling and the sirens wailing and something—either myself or else that other wooden body—begin to splinter.

II

Away From the Airport

The air-conditioning was broken. Arrivals smelled of toilets, and *somewhat* more poetically of rotting oranges, and I was still waiting for my luggage, which appeared to have been commandeered midway between the runway and reclaim. Also my arm was throbbing and had not stopped throbbing ever since the Montagnana had attacked me, and the remnants of its outburst kept seeping out and then congealing around the edges of my cast so that a little circle of goo now ringed the top of every finger.

Eventually my bags snaked round the metal belt and with a great deal of awkwardness I managed to manoeuvre them off it. Even here beneath the artificial lighting I could feel my skin beginning to freckle as if in anticipation of the August sun. I took out a bottle of sunblock and applied a thin white layer to any patch of myself that was exposed, then grabbed my other luggage and trundled into the outside glare.

"Ms Le Clef-" began the young woman, who was clutching a piece of paper with these same words on it.

"Allegra, please."

"Allegra. Eurydice. Your guide in Athens."

I looked down and saw two sticking plasters peeking out from the back of her patent high-heeled shoes and then as my gaze moved upwards that the matching belt that cinched the middle of her voluptuous body was held together with a rubber band.

"But where is Ivan? Eros said . . ."

"Mr Kamiński sends his regards. He arrived yesterday and is already waiting at the apartment but . . ." she took out her phone and started reading from the screen, "He doesn't see the point in coming to meet you all hot and bothered."

It was a typically Ivan-esque thing to say and yet it was not his words, mild by his usual standards, that bothered me.

"The apartment? So does that mean we're staying . . . *together*?"

"I am very sorry but no. As *Music Without Borders'* lead musician Mr Kamiński has sole use of the British Council apartment, but we have arranged a very nice Airbnb for you in downtown Athens. It's not quite as big but-"

"I'll be alone?"

"But I am very much looking forward to meeting with you both tomorrow and discussing your itineraries."

I wanted to say other professional sounding things—and to avoid hysteria, silence or further unnecessary reminiscences about my honeymoon—but Eurydice had already set off through the carpark. I stumbled after her and towards a once smart BMW burning with the heat. I waited as she unlocked the boot and with a force that surprised me threw my suitcase inside. Then she got in, kicked off her shoes and reached for a pair of sunglasses—huge wrap around ones with gold medusa heads emblazoned on the sides —while I stood and stared at the sweaty leather seats. And listened to my arm, still throbbing-

"Is something wrong?" said Eurydice.

"No. Sorry. I just- Flying always makes me feel a little . . . *unusual*."

I opened the door to the passenger side and got in next to her, taking care to spread my skirt so that any bare skin was protected by the cotton. The tarmac was sticky and the sky emitted a bright, polluted shimmer. I wound my window down but even when the car started moving there was barely any breeze. Hills and fields spread out on either side of the motorway but they were so dry that it would not have surprised me if everything as far as I could see caught fire and the tiny houses dotted in between the dusty mounds of earth had crumpled to ash in front of us . . .

"You have visited Athens before?" said Eurydice

"Yes. But a long time ago now."

"For work?"

"No."

She gave me a curious look but said nothing further. A few minutes passed and then she turned the radio on. A tinny warbling rose around us but drowned out in places by the engine. I listened as a woman implored a man to hold her, save her, and be saved by her, and watched as the fields turned into the suburbs and more and more square white buildings ate into the dried-up fields. I felt as if I was inside a music video made by an avant-garde artist and that someone at some point—perhaps even Albion—would let me in on the joke . . .

"It wouldn't normally take so long," said Eurydice. "But I have to pick up the keys and want I avoid the protests."

"Against the borders?"

To my surprise Eurydice burst out laughing.

"Yes, but not yours." Her tone changed to one that was kinder than I had expected. "It's nothing to worry about. But the police use teargas and it lingers in the air."

Feierliches Stück

I leaned my head out the window. I could hear my hair rustling like the wind that no longer existed. The song switched to one in which a man implored a woman not to leave him, and also to try to understand him, and a Greek DJ said several things I didn't understand. I realised that the countryside had disappeared completely and that there were now only tall white buildings standing in austere, blinding blocks. And then as we moved inside them they became increasingly dirty. And then increasingly haphazard, jumbled together until they left no room for anything else. And yet between them even dirtier more haphazard backstreets still sprang up. Eurydice kept on driving until she reached a tiny square filled with market stalls, pulled up beside a broken pillar and stopped.

I waited as she got out of the car and then once she was out of sight began to fiddle with the radio. There was more singing, some static, then *Feierliches Stück* from Lohengrin. I turned the volume up as high as it would go. On my right was a group of police officers, thickset moustachioed men with guns. On my left was a bric-a-brac stall. I got out of the car and went over to it and in an attempt to look purposeful picked up a wicker basket filled with jewellery. I extracted an enamel brooch, the sort of thing I might have used to 'lift' one of my more sombre evening dresses, and turned it over in my hand. Gold leaves curled around the edges and in the middle of them an eagle. I peered closer and saw that the eagle was carrying a red flag with a black swastika in the centre. I let out a little gasp.

"These days it's mainly Jews who collect them," said the seller in perfect English and then looking at me quizzically she added, "although some other types as well."

I nodded, put the brooch back in the basket and wanting to look busy took out my phone. I had two new emails, one from Albion and one from The_Saracens_79. I tapped on The_Sarcens_79 and read:

In answer to your earlier question, I would describe myself as 'centrist'. I believe in the virtues of capitalism and individual wealth, but I also believe that capitalism and economic prosperity should ultimately serve the needs of everybody, not just the few.

I think that banks, large corporations—any institutions that employ lots of people and are flush with cash—are morally and ethically compelled to contribute to the general living standards and spread-wealth of the countries they operate in. They can do this in all sorts of ways: investing in various social programs, government schemes . . .

"Miss? Miss? Please?"

I looked down to see a little girl tugging at my skirt. A bag of tissues—the kind that came in cellophane packets and women of a certain age supposedly liked to carry in their handbags—was looped over her arm while the hand that wasn't already attached to me was outstretched, palm upwards.

"Miss? Miss? Please, one euro . . ."

I took out my purse and then, remembering that I had not yet had time to take out any money immediately wished I hadn't. I tried to smile as I put it back inside my handbag. As I did so I became aware that the gunk around the edges of my cast seemed to be increasing as did the intensity of the throbbing.

"I'm sorry. I- I didn't realise. I- I-"

"Please Miss, one euro . . ."

"I- I- I-"

Her eyes were large and pleading but then, when I continued to stammer they slowly narrowed into slits. I could see that her hair was matted and also that she was extremely small in a disproportionate way that made it appear as though she was the wrong size for her age. I wondered if she had parents, and if not who sent her out with the tissues, as well as where she came from-

"I- I'm sorry . . ." I repeated.

"You waste my time Miss."

She let go of my skirt and stepped backwards into the gutter that was full of cigarette butts, then spat on the ground.

There was a pause and then with an older and more adult intonation, "Kos omak!"

"But I really am really sorry!"

But she had already darted off, weaving her way through the policeman's legs and disappearing into the dirty jumbled streets behind them.

A Child Can Drown in Two Inches of Water

I forgot about Wagner, which was still blaring from the car, and walked into what I now saw was a café situated on the far side of the square. I scanned the tables in search of a napkin – or a tissue – with which to try and clean my bloody fingers but saw nothing bar plump blonde families scooping ice-cream into their mouths. I waited until I thought that no one was looking and then attempted to wipe my fingers on the corner of one of the tablecloths. I managed to remove the goo from the first two before a waiter noticed. Again I took out my phone but this time tapped on Albion's message. Yet the words all seeped into each other until I was only aware of the following two sentences:

> . . . *Anker and I have been spending a lot of time together, and to be honest we have been getting pretty close. If you were here maybe this wouldn't be happening but as you know I am alone* . . .

I re-read them several times and the blood from my arm rose up and began to soak into my brain and then the sickness that nowadays was always with me rose up too. I could just about make out one of the police officers who appeared to be reprimanding one of the waiters and beside them a man with a shaved head who was examining the Nazi brooch. Then the little girl reappeared and began talking to a group of especially plump especially blonde ice-cream eaters and a man who looked like he could be their father handed her some money. The scent of toilets and rotting oranges returned burning deep inside my nostrils. Again I thought of fire, ash, and also dry bones lying in the desert. I remembered the English phrase 'It's all Greek to me'. I remembered that although there were numerous operas based on Greek mythology there were very few Greek operas-

"Allegra? Allegra, *please*," and I sensed that Eurydice was now beside me, the keys to something jingling in her hand, "Are you alright? *Allegra*?"

"I . . ."

I could see the little girl who had reappeared again looking at me with contempt. I reached for my purse, then remembered that I hadn't yet had time to take out any money. And then it was too hot to remember anything else except the car that was as slick and burning as the tarmac underneath it and that my brain and my arm were burning, or drowning, or dead.

Lithopaedion

Hours or possibly even days later I opened my eyes and blinked. Too bright, white light was streaming through the window onto the equally blinding sheets. My wrist was no longer encased in plaster but back in the support.

This time however it did not attempt to ape my own sickly flesh but was coloured a garish neon the same shade as the FEELINGS sculpture.

I turned to the Consultant and said, "You've got a beard."

"This is true," said the Consultant, and then, "My name is Dr Agrios."

I blinked again and the memory of my Montagnana and the pain that I had caused it came flooding suddenly, brutally back. I cried out with shame and covered my mouth with the sheet.

"Ms Le Clef-"

"Allegra, please."

"Is there pain, Allegra?"

"No," and then aware that what had until now only appeared to be a hopeless situation may actually have become one, "will there be? Will I- I-"

"Not necessarily, no. There is some, minor trauma to the bone but overall you have not increased the damage. You had an operation . . . ?"

I let go of the sheet.

"Yes, last week."

"Then you have no need to worry. Thing are progressing as they should and the bones will knit together, eventually. But the other matter . . ."

"The other matter?"

"Of your pregnancy."

A bag of fruit was lying on the table between the next patient and my bed. I grabbed then shook it so that a bunch of grapes fell out onto the floor and rolled across the marble like a broken necklace.

"It is lithopaedion," Dr Agrios continued and then, "can you breathe?"

I nodded but at the same time held the bag against my mouth.

"Do you know what lithopaedion means?"

"No." I looked at the grapes, one of which had already been squashed by a nurse's shoe. "I mean I- I- " I sucked from the bag again. "I didn't even know that I was pregnant."

"And did you want to be?"

"I don't think so. I mean I- we- my husband. We- we talked about it. But sometimes I'm so busy that I don't have time for breakfast, and if you have a child . . ."

"It needs breakfast?"

"No. Yes. I . . ."

"Well then no matter," and to my surprise he squeezed my hand. "You are not pregnant anymore. A lithopaedion, or stone baby as it is sometimes known, occurs when the foetus calcifies outside the womb-"

"So I have a stone inside me?"

"You have a calcified foetus in your abdomen, yes. But we can give you something to induce labour and-"

"I don't want another abortion."

"What?"

101

"It's nothing," and then I repeated to myself, *nothing*, and then out loud, "And you're sure that there is no extra damage. To my wrist?"

Beethoven's Third Sonata

I let my thoughts wander off into a strange, trance like place. I remembered the night of the accident. How usual meaning well the concert that I had given had gone and how usual meaning nondescript the journey home from it had been until the van pulled out in front of us. Afterwards one of the paramedics told me that I was lucky; they had thought that I might lose my legs. But although my body, my career, and possibly even my marriage could have survived without these unnecessary appendages – a fact that made me weep with rage - without my wrist, I was nothing . . .

I remembered Albion placing his hand upon my stomach and joking-not-joking that we should make a baby, which was the sort of joke that those with happy childhoods made. Of course there were other unhappy grown-up children who decided to play at families via accident or some other hormone fuelled mistake. But mistakes were not part of my repertoire. Nor sagging breasts and torn vaginas. And yet I had still laughed as though a baby was a real possibility, but now that possibility was nothing . . .

I remembered my fifteenth birthday. Up until that point apples had been the one 100 calorie food that I had always permitted myself to eat but on that day I had decided that I did not deserve to swallow until I had mastered Beethoven's third sonata which, faint with hunger, I had then eventually learnt to play. But how could I continue to swallow everything down when I was sick? But how could I be nothing and still continue to exist . . . ?

Obsolete

Yet a small sharp corner pressing into my thigh forced me back into the moment. I looked down and saw that Dr Agrios had begun to place a stack of what should have been obsolete CD cases on the bed as well as a marker-pen, the implication being that he wanted me to sign them. I peered more closely and the pale, oval face repeated across different but equally smooth decades stared blankly back. The same auburn waves flowed over the same ivory shoulders, the same-but-different taffeta dresses sparkled against the same-but-different black-out curtains, and my own name spelled out again and again in a variety of serif typefaces many of which were accented with further swirls and occasionally the name of an orchestra. Mentally I compared these images with the newest set of promotional photographs then wondered how much longer the record company could keep on retouching me before the discord between these flat and uniform surfaces and my present physical reality became apparent. I was now a dead star but the light emitted during my brief lifetime would continue its journey through space, and thus my former brilliance could, potentially, still be visible for years or possibly even centuries to come . . .

Etudes Boreales

"So do you play?"

My goal was not the answer, but to provide Dr Agrios with an opportunity to ask about my own career and in so doing to establish whether or not he had picked me to be his patient or if I had willed him with his black-eyed good looks and rich tenor voice to be my doctor. Before the accident I had believed that I was destined to repeat my successes and the style of them over and over—something that the CD cases also appeared to confirm—but had since come to fear that it was actually the same dis-eases that I was destined to repeatedly perform. I wanted confirmation that to those on earth my radiance, or the illusion of it, was still apparent, and so I waited with a stone growing inside my stomach for Dr Agrios to speak. There was a long silence during which he took out a packet of cigarettes and without asking if I minded lit one.

I continued waiting as he took a drag and then just when it was on the verge of being intolerable said,

"I did. Once. But not for many years. You see my father, he made his living as a chemist but music was his passion."

I scrawled my name across the first album cover then added a row of kisses underneath.

"I have always been jealous of those with passions," I said coldly.

"Really?" Dr Agrios looked surprised. "But your-"

"My Montagnana?" I shrugged, "That's kind of complicated."

Dr Agrios exhaled and then after a brief pause said, "What you mean I think is that you are jealous of those with one grand romantic passion that then consumes the rest. But in reality the one grand passion is unpleasant in that it destroys all of the other smaller ones that make life bearable and replaces them with something so huge and monstrous that it can never be fulfilled."

"But I had a grand passion - my husband," I replied automatically, but then as soon as I said it I realised that although I had said it—and thought it and felt it—I had never really done anything that might constitute an actual, concrete proof, "although now I'm dating a corporate lawyer. It's still early days, but we text each other every day," and then aware that I didn't want to pursue this path either, "but it really is the passions plural—the little things 'that make life bearable'—that I have always lacked."

"Of course. *Anyway*," Dr Agrios took another drag on his cigarette and clearly preferring his story to mine he continued, "my father played the kementse, a type of gypsy fiddle. He played at home and in the tavernas. He played in the mornings and the evenings and on Sundays, the one day when he shut up shop, he played in the afternoon too."

"So he played all day then?" I said, sullenly, disappointed that my plan had not worked.

"Yes, he played all day, and given the chance he would have played all night too," Dr Agrios carried on blithely, "yet by the age of five I was not only good enough to accompany him but also to compose small pieces. At eight I had surpassed him completely."

"And did he mind?" I said thinking of my own parents who, seeing me only as an extension of themselves, had only minded when I failed to bring home prizes, "Did he still continue to encourage you?"

"Yes of course. Whenever he was not working or practicing we would drive into the centre of Athens to listen to classical music. It was there that I first heard the cello. Shortly afterwards I began taking lessons. And then but a year later I applied and was accepted to a prestigious music camp. I flew to America in order to attend it and to spend my summer holidays with ten other children each one of whom had also been hailed as a great talent. And each day we practiced in our little cell like rooms and each evening we gave a concert for the teachers, during which a terrible fact emerged: that I was not the best. And so I became a doctor, which pays considerably better than being a chemist does."

"Oh . . . I mean I . . ."

"Anyway, I still enjoy listening to the cello very much. Actually, I have just discovered a new musician that I am very excited by."

Before I had time to say anything further he pulled out an iPod and once again without asking if I minded attached it to a pair of miniature speakers. He pressed play and a second later the composition began to zigzag about us like a fly.

"I don't normally like John Cage," Dr Agrios said happily, "too clever-clever for my tastes. But there's something about this young woman—Hui Yin I think is how you say it—which is so skilful, masterful even, that I just can't help but be impressed."

The First Cemetery of Athens

In the evening they administered the drugs. More time passed during which invisible pokers burned into my stomach. I groaned like an animal. More time passed and then I laid a bloody stone. I went to sleep. Woke-up. Spat out breakfast and left. But as soon as I was sure that nobody could see me I turned in the opposite direction to the Airbnb and sloped along the motorway instead. The heat made it especially unpleasant but I hoped that if I kept on going I might at some point reach the sea.

Yet half an hour went by and there was only tarmac. My skin was beginning to prickle, my garish arm already ached and I felt as if my insides had been ripped out, because they had. There was no shade just the cloudless sky and with the sun so far up that nothing cast a shadow. I passed the turning for a side street at the end of which I could see a flower stall covered by a large green awning. I walked towards it and asked the stall-holder, in English, if I could buy something to drink. She shook her head then gave me an old plastic bottle filled with lukewarm water. I drank the entire thing in one go and put the empty bottle in my bag. Feeling obliged to purchase something I selected an extravagant bouquet of roses. As I did so I noticed that most of the other arrangements were wreathes, and then that two wrought-iron angels towered above us. Suddenly, I understood why: I had reached the cemetery.

I entered through the gates and immediately found myself in the middle of a marble square that shone with a whiteness even brighter and more dazzling than that of the hospital. To my left was what looked like an orthodox church replete with dome, bell, and golden crucifix which, I assumed, must be a funerary chapel. Huge spotless tombs realised in a classical or perhaps totalitarian style surrounded it. I wondered if any of them housed famous people but as all of the writing was in Cyrillic I had no way of knowing for sure.

I held up my good hand to shade my eyes, and began to head towards the sinister calm of the Cyprus trees beyond. The further I went the narrower and more uneven the paths became while the trees that edged them also grew denser. Metal dumpsters appeared whenever one path ended or crossed with another, each of which was filled with withered flowers. Weeds grew from the burnt grass in front of the older less ostentatious graves but the newer ones had fresh bouquets as well as photographs and lanterns, many of which were burning.

Risqué

Every so often a stout, fifty-plus woman lumbered by in heavy looking clothes — some even wore tights — and yet they seemed unhindered by the heat. The only sounds that I could hear were pigeons cooing, the motorway, faint but persistent in the background, and occasionally the gush of running water. This came from taps dotted at regular intervals along the pathways. I watched as the women filled their buckets from them before returning to water the graves, then went and filled my own bottle, drank the warm but sparkling water and filled my bottle again.

In the distance I could see a large ancient tomb with a marble seat carved into it and a patch of nettles at the front. As no one else seemed interested in this part of the cemetery I went over and sat down. The surrounding Cyprus trees blocked out most of the light making it so dark that the bench was almost cool. I closed my eyes and breathed deeply. It was the first time since I had arrived that I had relaxed. Only-

PING! PING! PING!

I opened my eyes. I saw that I had one new message from The_Saracens_79 tapped on it and read, *Are you alone?*

I glanced at the old women who remained far away. I drank some more water looked at the wrist-support and then the bouquet of roses. I thought about my lack of a husband, my lack of friends, my lack of passions plural, and the parents that I had never really known. Then I texted, *Yes.*

A moment's silence and, *And you're open to something risqué?* pinged back.

I looked at the roses and the wrist-support. I drank some more water. And then I let my mind go blank. I thought of the fan letters that I had occasionally received the first one of which I had responded to with the line, 'You can't love me, because you don't know me.' Then I looked at the roses but not the wrist-support. Then, I realised that I had drunk all the water. I texted, *Yes.*

My phone started ringing. I looked at the roses and pressed answer.

"Allemande . . . ?"

The voice was older and plumier than I had expected, but it surprised me primarily because I had never thought about The_Saracens_79 in terms of sounds.

My mind went blank and my mouth went dry but I managed to croak, "Hello."

"So Allemande . . . What turns you on?"

"I . . ."

A mature but adolescent laughter and of the type that called to mind a private, possibly single sex, education greeted my uncertainty. I noticed that the roses were wilting.

Then The_Saracens_79 stopped laughing and said, "Now come on Allemande, don't be shy. I want to know your fantasy."

"Well . . ." I said nervously, blankly, but then a new thought occurred, "Well I err, I like to imagine that I'm back at school. And I'm err, I'm wearing a school uniform, you know the type of thing, white blouse, pleated skirt, only it's all too tight for me. My breasts are practically falling out of it . . ."

I paused and tried to remember what had happened next.

"Go on," said the voice, which now sounded only young and eager.

"Well I err, I have to go and see my err, my music teacher and ask, no err beg, beg him not to fail me, because you know, I've been really bad and err, not done my homework, yes that's it, I've not done my homework, and that means that I might not pass my exams. And so I plead with him for ages and ages, only it makes no difference, but then, just when it looks like he's had enough and is going to throw me out, he picks up a ruler, slaps it against his palm, and says, 'You want to pass so bad? I want to see just how bad you really want to pass!' "

"Go on," said the voice, which had now dropped to a whisper.

"Well ... I'm scared, but I'm also really turned on by err, by like his strictness, and his authority and err, stuff. So I nod, and then I lift up my skirt and lie down across the desk, and then he err, well . . ." I struggled to hold back the laughter that was also panic and then when I had regained my composure said, "He, err, he begins to spank me. And every time the ruler hits my buttocks he asks me what else I'm prepared to do. Am I prepared to go before the school board for example? And then—because even though it hurts and I'm humiliated and exposed and err, everything, it also makes me wet and err, like really ready, really like aching to be fucked—I say 'Yes! Yes! Anything!' And then he asks, 'But are you prepared to really work for it?' And then-"

"I'm going to fill all your holes."

I stopped abruptly as a particularly stout old woman walked up to a neighbouring grave and turned on one of the taps while at the same time considering what the man who was now breathing very heavily into my right ear had just said. Was he, The_Saracens_79, really prepared to do this? To pack my wounds? To seal me? Stop me? Fill me up? I listened, both to his breath and to the sound of running water and then as the blood began to trickle down my thigh I pondered what if anything I could offer him in recompense for this kindness . . . ?

"Go on," and now the voice was frantic, insistent and could have belonged to any man of any age.

"Oh err, yes, well then they, the, err, the school board, all come in, and gather around me except that now I've err, yes, yes sorry I forgot to say that just before they came in, I took off all my clothes and now I'm err, I'm crouched, on top of the desk, and err yes, I'm naked, totally naked, with all my hair all over my face. And then they, the, err, the school board, all get their dicks out, and all their dicks are really massive, and even though I can't really see their faces, or tell whose dick is whose I start to suck them. In fact, I'm really, really desperate to suck them all, and to suck up all their cum, and have them cum on my face and in my hair, and err, and on everything until I'm practically swimming in it. And so I just keep on, moving back and forth between them all and sucking all their different, massive dicks. And sometimes they, the err, the school board, they grab me by my hair, and push their dicks even further down my throat so that I start choking, but by that point I'm so fucking turned on that there's no way I can stop. And because they know this they just keep on pushing. And slapping me on my slutty little legs. And telling me how much they want to see me work it. And I can feel their fingers sliding in and out my cun- I err, I mean my pussy, which is so, so wet right now. And then they like, oh yeah, I err, I forgot to say that then they tie me up. They tie my hands and my wrists together and then the whole thing is all about my arse. And even though I still can't see their faces, and still can't even tell who is doing what to me, I just love it and I want it and I can't stop fucking moaning and begging them to fuck me, even though sometimes it sounds a bit like I'm actually crying. And then, just when I reach a point where I've practically passed out from pleasure and just err, just generally being a whore, all the attention switches to my arsehole, and I hear a voice saying, 'Yeah. That's right. Open her up.'"

Eureka!

I caught a taxi back to the apartment where Eurydice had not only taken my luggage but also unpacked it for me and by the look of it ironed my clothes. The grey silk wrap was now smooth again and draped artfully across a padded hanger, a new swimming costume— green of course, because green was a mermaid's colour —twisted jauntily behind it, and a pair of ribbon-tie sandals bought many years ago in anticipation of drinks and dancing stood poised expectantly beneath.

I returned to the living area and opened my laptop but instead of checking my emails I ordered a pair of gold high-heeled sandals and a gold silk dress to match them. I had just typed in my card details when my handbag started ringing. I took out my phone and—almost relieved to see that the screen displayed Ivan's name—pressed answer. I braced myself and then-

"I am very disappointed."

I held the phone so that it was a few inches from my ear and said, "Of course you are."

"I can't hear you. Please speak up Allegra, or is even that too much trouble?"

I moved the phone an inch closer.

"Of . . ."

"I said speak up!"

"Of course you are!"

"Well really Allegra, there is no need to shout. All you need to say is sorry."

I rammed the phone against my cheek smearing the screen with a combination of sweat and suntan lotion.

"I'm not going to apologise for being ill."

"Even if the illness was your fault?"

"I . . ."

I knew that both of the things that I had missed —a visit to a school followed by a British Council dinner—had been minor ones and also that had Ivan known the extent of my problems then he would have (hopefully) been kinder. But I still couldn't bring myself to mention that other, verging on major, thing that had weighed me down without my knowing and then morphed into another more fluid kind of curse. For a second I forgot that there was someone on the other end of the phone and thought only of my Montagnana and how much I wanted to hold it in my arms before remembering that it was also sick. I thought of how the seat beside me on the plane, which would usually have been filled either by it or Albion, had remained as empty as I was now and then asked myself who or what could ever fill this emptiness . . .

"I mean, what do you want me to do?" I said irritably, "Besides sit here and listen to you harangue me?"

Momentarily there was silence.

"Eureka-"

"Eurydice?"

"The chubby girl with the sticking plasters?"

"She's not-"

"Overweight? Well, I told her to reschedule our meeting for tomorrow. We will now meet then instead and she will explain how *you*" and there was a pause into which I could sense that he was jabbing his finger, "can assist *me*."

Curdling

I rooted through the few unfashionable items that still remained in the bottom of my suitcase until I found my flannelette pyjamas. I put them on and wandered into the kitchen. Like all of the apartment's rooms the shutters had been drawn until the evening and what little light there was fell in between the slats turning each wall into a feverish, zebra printed pattern. I was too hot. I removed my pyjamas and stood there, naked but for the knickers that the hospital had provided and then stuffed with giant, what I thought of as industrial, sanitary pads.

After a while I opened the cupboard nearest to me and took out a box of loose-leafed tea. I made a pot with lemon but no milk, which I could not think even think of without thinking of it curdling. I could hear although not see a mosquito buzzing and I could see although not hear something, most likely washing, brushing back and forth against the shutters. I went back into the living area, picked up my phone and saw that Ivan had murdered the battery. I turned my handbag upside down and shook it. Crumpled receipts and pieces of chewing gum fell out onto the floor but not the charger.

I wandered out into the hall where I remembered seeing a landline and called Verity, first on her mobile and then on her home number, and then against my better judgement I phoned Hale. He had always irritated me but since the accident my original annoyance had turned into a hate so pure that had I not been tied to Verity then I would have openly wished him dead. A dull ringing sounded in my ears. Again there was no answer. Exhausted, I returned to the living area. My hate became weariness became sleep. And as I lay upon the sofa what little parts of me remained drifted into nothing . . .

Fire!

When I woke the heat had dropped. I washed, and changed my sanitary pad before retrieving my flannelette pyjamas. I went back to the kitchen and this time found a loaf of bread, a tin of sardines, and the remaining half of a lemon. I had just opened the sardines when the landline started ringing but which, not thinking that it would be for me, I ignored. I cut a slice of bread as it switched to voicemail and then as a Greek woman made a Greek apology I popped it in the toaster.

There was a moment's silence and another, English voice began to speak, "Allegra. Hale here. I got your message and-"

But before he had time to go any further I had already dashed into the hallway and picked up the phone.

"Hale? Hale?! You still there?!"

"I'm still here, I-"

"It's Allegra. And I'm in Greece. In Athens. I'm err- I'm actually helping Ivan. Not right now obviously, but soon. Although since I got here I've been feeling a bit . . . *unusual*. Actually, I've not been well-"

"Neither has Verity," Hale cut in, "I mean you must have noticed the juicing-"

"How could I not," and I laughed, perhaps a little too shortly, at his perpetual dumbness, "That and the bloody yoga. What's next – colonic irrigation? But the thing is I'm actually calling about something important-"

"As am I." I waited and then, "Verity's not here. She's in the country. And the place she's staying doesn't allow mobile phones. I'm driving up to join her after dinner and . . . You see the- the thing is . . ."

"The thing is what Hale?" I said sharply.

"Verity's not been well-"

"Yes, we've established that."

"And now she's gone somewhere where she can be looked after, somewhere where- You see the thing about the hos-"

A long piercing beep sounded from the kitchen. I dropped the receiver and ran towards it. Smoke was pouring out the toaster, which in turn had set off the fire-alarm. I switched off the toaster, wafted a piece of newspaper underneath the fire-alarm and then ran back into the hallway.

I picked up the phone and over the beeping shouted, "Somethings come up. Just ask Verity to call

119

me when she gets back, okay? And in the meantime you might want to think about- what's that thing they say now? 'Man-up'? Well you might want to think about 'maning-up' and-"

"Allegra! *Please*. What I'm trying to tell you is-"

But the beeping wouldn't stop and the thought that I needed to stop it was filling me with panic. And this together with the tightness in my chest and the pain inside my empty holes was enough to make me think that I would faint. I had wanted Verity to help me but she was on a yoga retreat that did not allow mobile phones. I had wanted Hale to let me talk to her but he refused. I had wanted Albion, my husband, to take me as far away from me as was possible to go, to tell me that it didn't matter about my wrist or the possibility of our baby that had died; but at the same time I wanted him to stay away forever and forget that I existed . . . I had wanted and I had wanted but no one gave me what I wanted because on some deep and fundamental level I had always lacked, and all the while the stupid frenzied beeping-

"Hale!" I shouted, my voice rising to the same shrill pitch as the alarm, "For once in your life please listen and even if you'll always be too much of a coward to apologise then at least just try to understand. I have not got time for this. I. Have. Not. Got. Time."

Ravel

I strode round the apartment, looking. Although I wasn't entirely sure what for. There was an antiquated stereo in the bedroom. I turned the dial, trying to find Radio Three but hoping that something other than *Choral Evensong* would be playing. Yet there was only static. I carried on turning, looking, finding nothing until I eventually chanced upon a Radio Four documentary. The presenter listed the numerous oppressive regimes that Britain had supplied with weapons. She interviewed several politicians all of whom came across as vague and not particularly bothered. Then several activists who blazed with anger and confusion. I wanted to side with the activists but suspected that they might wear rainbow clothes. Then I went back into the kitchen and opened the sardines.

And then I took a deep, deep breath and flung the shutters open. And then the doors to the balcony where I felt the heat of the sun faintly smouldering at the evening's edges. Although the street on which I was staying was, like all the streets, rundown the little courtyard behind the apartment block was scrupulously clean. Every balcony was covered in a striped awning and housed wrought iron chairs and tables, and the little square beneath was full of lush and very well-tended pot plants. A fat old man dozed on the balcony directly opposite and skinny mottled kittens played on the roof above him.

I put my dinner on the table and sat down on one of the matching chairs. Straight away a terrible wailing started. At first I thought it was another alarm then realised that it was the kittens who could smell my sardines and were now crying out for them. They ran across the rooftop, every so often stopping and almost jumping off it before deciding that it was too far and at the last minute drawing back. Then the largest one jumped down onto one of the nearer balconies wailing even louder than before while the others also raised their voices as if in sympathy until they formed a choir.

Of course I myself had perfect pitch yet seldom sang out loud. I had always preferred my cello's voice to any human's but didn't see this preference as being in any way problematic primarily because it was one that most composers seemed to share. I had only played cello obbligato once on a recording of *Chansons Madécasses* and the opening of the second song, *Aoua!* Had made me feel so ill that I refused to even to listen to it afterwards. I stood up holding the plate out in front of me as I did so, so that the sardines were even closer to the kittens who immediately increased in volume as a result, and then I began to sing realising as I did so that for some unknown reason I still remembered every word.

What I lacked in range I more than made up in emotion, or feelings even, and as the feelings got louder so did I. The old man woke up and looked at me, confused. But still I carried on singing. Then he started shouting, then went inside and slammed the door - but still I carried on. I could hear the landline ringing inside the apartment but I ignored it and then once again the smoke alarm screaming for my attention. But still I carried on and on - relentless in my emotion. I thought of the little refugee girl and how small and dirty she was. Of the weapons that my sinking, stinking island sold to Syria and of the embarrassing rainbow people who opposed them-

"Mefiez-vous des blancs," I sang or maybe shouted and then just in case anyone who might have heard me hadn't, "MEFIEZ-VOUS DES BLANCS!"

On Repeat

But at some point it ended. I slept again. Then woke the following lunchtime and having no escape routes left took a taxi to the cafe where Ivan was lying in wait. Despite the early hour he had already ordered an appropriately cloudy glass of ouzo and was half way through a packet of his Polish cigarettes, while Eurydice who was sitting beside him toyed with long white menthol without appearing to inhale. Her manner was so languid but at the same time provocative that it reminded me of Scarlett. She was not chubby I though defiantly. She was charming-

"Do I disgust you?" said Ivan, who I had clearly annoyed not by my strained expression but by

the fact that my focus had already shifted away from him and towards another. "Am I too much for your sensitive stomach?"

"Yes you do." I sat down on one of the wooden seats opposite, "But in a strange way it's comforting."

Sarcasm had been my intention and I could tell from Ivan's downturned mouth that I had succeeded in fulfilling it and yet what I had said was also true. Our relationship was almost as dysfunctional as the one with my own parents had been both in that Ivan had at times lived precariously through me and that even after all these years I could not be sure what was love and what was all I knew. Looking down at my FEELINGS coloured wrist-support I thought back to the concert and the unexpected kindness with which he had treated Verity. He would never have subjected her to the same rude behaviours that he sometimes did me mainly because she lacked my talent, just as I would never have belittled him the way I did her because I knew that deep down no one else was more appreciative of my skill. I thought, he only hurts me because he loves me. And then, he only hits me because he loves me. And then I pictured myself saying 'hit me' and Albion reluctantly obliging, my body crumpling against the car's metal bonnet, and the clouds of ouzo, rising upwards with the smoke-

"Hit me God, please hit me," I said, but by mistake out loud.

124

"Are you attempting to be interesting?" said Ivan.

"I . . ."

"You?"

"Or both of us-"

But then I stopped myself before doing something that everyone regretted.

Crawl

I made a few attempts at polite conversation for Eurydice's sake, then took my new and vastly reduced itinerary, which was now entirely devoid of either dinner parties or school visits, and returned to the Airbnb. Then I stuffed my swimming things into a bag and set off through the now even hotter even stiller air. I had been told that the pool was only a few minutes walk away and yet each step of my journey dragged as if like yesterday I had been lost upon the road. By the time I reached my destination—a large, neoclassical building flanked by rows of pillars—my mouth was parched. Through the glass I could see the cool blue water, only it wasn't water I could drink.

I went up to the desk and said, "One for adult lane swim please."

"I need to see your certificate," said the Receptionist, who was seated in such a way that she blocked the entrance to the pool *and* the adjoining café, "No one is allowed in without one."

Assuming that it was her perfect English that was at fault and that what she actually meant was passport I found and then held out this item.

"No, from the Doctor."

"You need a certificate about my wrist?"

"No, your feet. I need proof that you do not have verrucas."

Obviously I did not have verrucas because obviously I was not that sort of person but the feeling of blood clotting on the cotton pad between my legs was enough to persuade me that this was not a fact worth fighting for. I looked back into the pool and the lean stretched out limbs of one person trailing on from another. A woman almost entirely submerged beneath the water appeared to float over the receptionist's head. There was hardly any friction as she moved and although I was too far away to hear anything I was sure that even up close her body made no sound.

I swallowed and said, "What about a glass of water? Do I need a certificate for that?"

Before

I passed through the café and onto the marble terrace then sat on a plastic chair in front of a plastic table. The Waitress who was stacking cups together appeared to be completely absorbed by this task and thinking that it would be some time before she came to take my order I took the opportunity to check my emails. There was only one, from Albion, which I deleted without reading. Then I wondered whether or not he was sleeping with Anker yet and retrieved it from the deleted folder. Then immediately deleted it without reading it again . . .

I laid my phone face down upon the table and thought about how despite my best attempts to hide it I had always had competition and Albion had not. He had not been single when I met him whereas I had been for over a year and his relationships, unlike mine, had always overlapped. His first serious romance had been with Marie-Fleur, a redhead whom he had met during his gap year in Provence. She had then been usurped by Petronella, a redhead whom he had studied with at the Courtauld. She had then given way to Camilla, a redhead with a trust fund and a passion for French bulldogs. And then me. In direct contrast my previous entanglements had consisted of Sebastian, a smallish pianist with a small penis — which had it actually been a joke would have made me laugh instead of grit my teeth — followed eight months later by Conrad-Boy who before the alcoholism took hold had aspired to composition.

In the past I had clung to a memory from my green and jasmine-scented honeymoon when Albion had said that no one else had ever made him feel more alive, but now that Athens was a dried-up ruin I asked myself whether feeling alive was the same as feeling happy. I had cut my thighs to feel alive, present, real and because I had not been happy. I had needed rather than enjoyed the pain; a reminder that death existed but which at the same time kept me at a distance from it. Did I too make Albion more aware of death? Could I ever be more to him than the postcard on the doormat? The trampled catalogue pages? The disfigured Rossetti (none of which had any contemporary significance in the art world anymore)?

Greek Roses

I sighed, then ran my finger over the ring of an ancient coffee stain while thinking somewhat absently of arse-holes. The area was not one that many tourists favoured, which should have meant no beggars and no guilt. Nevertheless a little girl—perhaps the same little girl as before?—now wriggled over the terrace wall, her small arms wrapped around a bucket of roses.

She sidled up to me, tugged at my sleeve and said, "Miss, miss, please, three euro."

I reached inside my purse and now that it was filled with the correct currency extracted a ten euro note.

"Here."

"You want three roses?"

"No, one is fine."

"But I have no coins?"

"It's fine, keep it."

Her whole face brightened—as quickly as it may or may not have darkened once before—allowing me to at least temporarily believe that those seven extra euros might really be enough to make a difference to her wasted life. I watched as she darted off, shouting something I didn't understand to someone outside my frame of vision and then the moment passed and the awfulness, the reality, overcame me. I turned my phone over and googled 'refugee charities' and a bottomless pit of hyperlinks appeared. I stared at them for a second then pushed my phone away. Then I worried lest another refugee might see my phone and try to steal it and quickly put it back inside my handbag . . .

The Same

"Miss? Are you ready to order?" said the Waitress, who had finally finished with the cups.

"A sparkling water. And a coffee. Please."

"Okay, so that's one sparkling water and one coffee?"

I nodded, she left, and a tall, blonde couple sat down next to me. They were young, tanned, healthy—a fact that was accentuated by their freshly ironed pastel shirts—and it was clear from the way that they kept touching each another that they were newly in love. I averted my eyes until the Waitress returned with my drinks but as she placed them on the table the couple turned and nodded in my direction.

"Ett mousserande vatten. Och en kaffe" said the woman to the man.

"A sparkling water. And a coffee. Please," said the man to the Waitress.

"Det samma?" said the woman.

"Oh yes, the same for me," said the man.

"Okay, so that's two sparkling waters and two coffees?"

They nodded, the Waitress left and I took a sip of water if not exactly enjoying then certainly enlivened by the faint prickling sensation that it produced. I looked at the rose in front of me and thought of the cemetery and the dirty desperate little girl and then, once I was sure that they had turned away again, I looked at the good-looking couple's very straight backs. I thought about Sweden's Nazi past, and how the chief of human rights' had recently expressed concern about their asylum laws, which were shocking. And then I remembered a concert that I had given the Royal Swedish Opera and how much I had enjoyed the applause

You Must Eat

I set my alarm for six the following morning and wanting to make the most of the brief, relative cool I washed and dressed as soon as I awoke. I checked the directions, picked up my handbag, and then as an afterthought removed my phone and placed it on the pillow.

Outside the streets were deserted bar the cats that slinked between them or else morphed into velvet cushions on the doorsteps. This time though they were silent and if I tried to pet them they bolted. When I looked upwards I saw the remains of trees cutting into the sky. Occasionally a crumpled ball, an orange that had died and then withered on the branch, dangled from it. Black flags hung from houses with slogans spray-painted on the walls beneath them in alphabets I had not seen before.

I stopped outside the only place that was open. The food was lined up in the window with the owner perched on a stool beside it. I looked at the sandwiches and bowels of tapioca and pistachio and the miniature Ferris wheel that when it turned crushed ripe oranges into juice.

Leaning in through the hatch I said, "What is there for breakfast?"

"Greeks don't have breakfast," said the owner, of course in English, then pointed to the spinach pie, "But if you are hungry, the spanakopita is always good."

"Okay spanakopita it is," and then, contemplating her previous statement, I added, "Maybe if I lived here I could be a decent mother - although I suppose that I'd still have to make it lunch."

"If you are expecting a child then you must eat."

"I . . ."

But before I could come up with a suitable explanation she had put two slices of spanakopita in a bag and also filled a plastic cup with juice. Not knowing what else to do I paid for both and said goodbye. Up ahead there was a small square covered in broken mosaics with graffitied benches positioned around the sides. I went and sat on one of them and took out the first spanakopita. The pastry was folded into greasy layers between which the spinach and feta had been compacted into a dense green mass. I held it up to my nose, breathing in the smell of olive oil as well as cigarettes and urine; a combination that reminded me how close to death I was, or alternatively that I was hungry and alive.

Hotel

It still took some time to find the former hotel because it looked so similar to all the other low-rise blocks that bordered it. The walls had been covered in a pale apricot stucco, now grimy around the bottom floors, and a trellis woven with dead plants was attached to one of the sides. A group of children playing ballgames on the steps stared at me as I approached. I tried to smile and then rattled the grill that was half drawn across the entrance. I could see the room behind it and a table where two blonde women in jeans and tee-shirts were sitting.

I pried the grill apart, squeezed through, then smoothed my hair and said, "I called last night. About volunteering."

The taller blonde ran her finger down a list sellotaped to the monitor in front of her.

"Allegra?" she said with an Australian accent.

"Yes I'm Ms- I mean yes, I'm Allegra."

"And is there anything in particular that you'd like to help us with Allegra?"

"Oh, whatever's easiest."

She nodded at the shorter blonde who then got up and holding her hands against the side of her mouth in an approximation of a megaphone shouted, "Mohammed!" and then, "Mohammed! Mohammed! Mohammed . . ." as the word echoed back and forth across the stairwell.

I looked up and saw row after row of peach coloured doorways running across the floors above us. I wondered how many refugees occupied each bedroom and how many had a bathroom of their own. For a moment I thought that I could hear more children but when I listened harder I heard heavy footsteps only. Then a young man appeared. He was also dressed in jeans and a tee-shirt but had dark hair and the same delicate bone structure as one or both of the little girls who had accosted me.

"Allegra is a volunteer," said the shorter blonde.

"She can help you with the breakfasts," said the taller one.

"But I didn't think that Greeks ate breakfast," I said attempting to be funny.

"Well you don't have to eat it if you don't want to," said the shorter one.

"I don't think that's what she meant," said the taller one.

"Yes, what I meant was-"

"Well, I'm from Aleppo," Mohammed broke in, in a faintly transatlantic accent, "And let me assure you, we definitely eat breakfast there."

"Then I'd be a bad mother in Syria!" I said brightly.

"What?" said the shorter blonde.

"Have you brought your children with you?" said the taller one.

"No, no I just meant that- oh it's nothing."

The Women in the Kitchen

I followed Mohammed into what had once between the hotel dining room and then realised that I was still carrying my now empty cup of juice. I looked around me for a bin but couldn't see one, only large, circular tables with office chairs tucked underneath. There was a pile of board games and other children's' toys piled up in one far corner and stacks of plates covering the window ledge behind me.

I put down my cup, picked up one of the plates and said, "Should I set the table?"

"Oh yeah, yeah thanks. If you do that I'll start the coffee."

Mohammed went over to what had once been the bar. A row of high stools remained and there were wine glasses hanging from the ceiling but all of the alcohol had been removed and replaced by a giant spluttering urn. I watched as he began to fiddle with the settings and after a minute or so I started laying out the plates. Then I began to look for knives and forks, only I couldn't see any.

"Where do I find cutlery?" I said.

"In the kitchen," and he pointed to a door at the opposite side of the room, "They'll show you what to do."

I did as he instructed, and entered what was still most definitely a kitchen. A group of women were clustered around a metal island in the centre. They wore headscarves and spoke to each other in a language or maybe several languages that I had never heard in any opera and so could not pretend to understand. In front of them were dozens of small bowls filled with olives, peppers, and hummus. One woman was grinding spices with a pestle and mortar, another was mashing fava beans, another preparing a salad. Watching them I became intensely conscious of my hair, which had gathered in a hot frizz around my shoulders. I began to pull it back into a rubber band only the music, which had suddenly started playing, distracted me in part because it used a Byzantine scale that I struggled to relate to-

"Welcome," said the woman who had been grinding spices.

"Hi," I said, noticing that all the others had now stopped what they were doing too.

"Where are you from?" said the woman who had been mashing fava beans.

"How long will you be with us?" said the woman who had been preparing a salad.

"And why are you here?" said someone who could have been anyone, "Do you have a job? Or a reason?"

"England. A week or so. Yes," and then, "at the conservatoire," and then even more hesitantly, "I'm a music- a music teacher.

I resumed tying up my hair but pulled too tight at the rubber band so that it snapped painfully across my scalp. The music grew louder, weirder, more ecstatic. I remembered my empty plastic cup on the shelf where the plates had been and thought of the urn, spluttering . . .

"I used to be a teacher," said the woman who was now once again making a salad.

"Mohammed used to be a lawyer," said the woman who had now run out of un-mashed beans.

136

"Speaking of whom," I broke in quickly, "He asked me to lay the table."

Breakfast

I returned to what was once again a dining room only my arms were filled with bags of pitta breads instead of knives and forks. I removed the packaging then placed them in the wicker baskets that Mohammed now provided. I saw that my plastic cup had been removed and that there were rows of mugs filled with coffee on top of the bar. A few families were already sitting at the tables and I could hear other ones making their way from the upper floors. I picked up a stray teddy that was lying on the ground and returned it to the corner with the toys. As I approached a little boy who had already taken up residence there gurgled something at me. I opened my mouth to reply but then not knowing whether or not I should speak to him in English turned back towards the bar.

"Sit down, have a coffee," said Mohammed, as if my awkwardness amused him, "The food won't be long."

"But I'm a volunteer."

"And a guest."

Reluctantly I sat down with one of the families and watched as the women from the kitchen began to file in together. As soon as they put down the bowls that they were carrying the families began to eat. They tore off pieces of the pitta bread and used it to scoop the food into their mouths. Not wanting to appear greedy I held back but then when I realised that no one was paying any attention to me I quickly followed suit. I completely forgot about the spanakopita and heaped my plate with so many things that one would have thought that it was I and not them who had nearly starved. But then again at one point I nearly had. At first each mouthful made me feel as though my stomach, my womb, was being mended, and then as if I were swallowing stones. But still I kept on, stuffing myself without ever feeling full. I decided that from now on I would take all my meals at the Refugee Centre and only when I was as heavy as what had nearly been my baby would I have given enough of myself to justify returning to the world.

Meandros

It took a few days more days until my penance was complete and convinced that a little of my privilege was now concealed behind a little layer of fat I made a faux-apologetic call to Eurydice. Under her instruction I then took a taxi to another small taverna outside of which she and Ivan were eating sweet syrup soaked pastries. A crumpled copy of my new and even more reduced itinerary lay between us with all of the appointments that I had missed so far circled in red biro.

In as calm a voice as possible I said, "But I'll still be there for *your* masterclass," knowing that my presence as Ivan's assistant would form a central part of his enjoyment. "*I* will still be there to support *you*."

"I have also been asked to give a lecture," said Ivan.

"And I'll be there for it."

"Of course you'll be there for it," he continued, petulantly, "And you will also read through my notes once Eureka leaves."

I watched as Eurydice smiled once again in the exact same languid, teasing way that Scarlett would have done had she been here now. Was I always drawn to the same type of people? I wondered. Or did everyone belong to one of the same not so varied types of which my own oft repeated neuroses were a symptom? Under Verity's guidance—or insistence—I had once been made to complete a Meyers-Briggs personality test which, after a hundred-and-fifty extremely boring questions, had labeled me an INFP. Yet even though the test had appealed to my vanity by concluding that idealism was in fact my biggest strength it had still not appealed to me generally, mainly because I could not imagine anyone other that the most ordinary type of person ever paying attention to it. I took a bite from one of the pastries and the syrup splurged down my chin and onto my plate. Sticky gold blobs fell across the black meandros border and a co-ordinating wasp began to drown.

- the Terrible

Suddenly my skin, my hair, my mouth were dry as a sandstone cave.

I turned to Eurydice and said, "Is there time to go swimming? Before the masterclass? I don't have a certificate but- but *please*."

"I'll see what I can do," said Eurydice.

"After we have gone over my notes," said Ivan.

"I . . ."

"You?"

"Us."

Eurydice shook her head and returned to the itinerary and the logistical requirements of the masterclass, the lecture, and going swimming regardless of verrucas until having sated both of us she excused herself and said goodbye. She paid our bill as she was leaving but forgot her cigarettes which, as soon as she was out of sight Ivan reached for. He took a drag and grimacing at the minty taste immediately stubbed it out on top of the drowning wasp.

"So now we will discuss *my* talk at the Conservatoire," he said, "so, please tell me, what would you advise?"

"I . . ." I began and then as was now usual stopped.

Because this one word on which I always faltered seemed to say everything there was to say about the singularity and self-obsession of my existence. I looked at Ivan who had always been older than me but younger than my parents and yet had always been the same wrinkled and leathery red-brown. I waited as he reached for and then lit one of his own Polish cigarettes and we were both enveloped by a toxic cloud of smoke, and thought about how he would always be there, just as ancient and ageless; a splinter in my starving heart . . .

"I would tell them that there is no point continuing unless you believe that you can be the best," and I breathed in his dirty air. "That it is not a love of music, but an obsession with winning that matters. And that history remembers the victors, not the fallen.

Arcadia

After Ivan had taken what he wanted I wandered towards the National Gardens. The road that led me there was filled with stalls selling Greek newspapers, drinks, and postcards. I examined one of a stone statue with a muscular body and a partly eroded face, one of a newly restored temple, and one of the colosseum. After some deliberation I opted for the statue on the grounds that its condition if not medium bore some relation to the portrait in Albion's study. Then I reached inside my handbag, pulled out a pen and put it in my mouth. I sucked thoughtfully. Some time passed and then:

Dear Albion,

Greetings from the National Gardens where the sun is shining very brightly. I can see (and hear!) tortoises making love and someone – I like to think a gypsy – is playing a kementse. Ivan has been behaving himself, although I suspect there's something brewing for my masterclass—which has turned him into a green-eyed monster—but at least it'll be over by Wednesday.

Until then kisses,

Allegra

I wrote down the Museum's address, as opposed to his apartment's in the hope that Anker might see it too, and then attached a second class stamp to the corner. Ideally I would have liked to have attached a third class one had third class ones existed. That way I would have still been able to send it and know that I had fulfilled my wifely duties but also that it would be several days or possibly even weeks before I would have to deal with the consequences of its arrival, not least of which would be the continuation of our correspondence.

Permission

The following day Eurydice picked me up in the BMW although this time we were heading out of and not into the city. The further we went the more affluent our surroundings became. Huge modernist villas rose out of the fossilised ruins and in between them futuristic, half-built structures jutting out over the water. The front and back walls which were, presumably, intended to be filled with glass were currently empty however, framing the sea in a series of perfectly composed panoramas.

Looking through them and into the water I said, "What will they become?"

"Nothing," said Eurydice shortly, "either the investors ran out of money, or their designs were illegal."

"Illegal?"

"It isn't safe to build so close to the shore. The developers began before they had obtained planning permission and then when they didn't get it had to stop. It's the same with most things here."

I turned from the blue sea to the black glasses trying to gage the expression that lay beneath them, but they were too dark and too thick to give anything away. In the wing-mirror I could see both Eurydice's and my hair billowing. We rounded a bend in the road and what I took to be a luxury hotel hove into view. The tiered terrace housed several swimming pools shining like jewels amidst the scorched earth while taught beige women with the type of skinniness that could only be paid for lay draped around the sides-

"But there still seems to be some money?"

"There still is some money," said the still inscrutable Eurydice, then laughed a feral Scarlett laugh, "It's just that very few people have it. And the Greek psyche is not attuned to poverty or to any form of puritanism. We like to dress well, to eat well, to drink, and as you have surely noticed to smoke."

"Even the staff at the hospital smoked. Even worse than Ivan."

She laughed again but the opportunity for gossip had already passed as the road ahead now took up all of her attention. She craned her head out of the window and reversed ten meters. Then swung round into the small turning that a moment earlier we had missed. As she did so two motorcyclists whizzed past us and at top speed rounded the first of the track's hairpin bends. Neither of them were wearing a helmet. Both had cigarettes in their mouths, and one of them was also holding a can of beer. They looked carefree and young in a way that I had never experienced. They reminded me that I was still sick.

Wedding Ring

Eurydice pulled over and reached for her bag. It was made of padded leather, slightly scuffed around the edges, and housed the what I now viewed as obligatory packet of menthols, broken Kirby-grips, and several pieces of greenish-tinged gold jewellery. I waited as she reapplied her lipstick and then followed her as she got out of the car and began to descend the flight of steep, wooden steps that were now directly in front of us. Rocks with rugged, coral like markings dropped sharply round the sides. More of the same coral hills stretched out above them for what seemed like forever and underneath the turquoise water; plus parasols and sun-loungers and smart starched waiters carrying trays of cocktails or else coffee with koulouria.

There was also a changing area hidden behind a large fence. Again I followed Eurydice as she went behind it and taking my cue from her began to remove my clothes. I had always been curious about other women's bodies and often imagined my own expensively scented and powdered flesh set in relief against the unapologetic Stilton of Hampstead's other early morning swimmers, Verity's fresh-faced yoga glow, or Scarlett's gym-toned midriff; all of which served the same purpose, namely to confirm that I was either normal or better via an endless process of comparison.

Yet as soon as I stole my first glance in Eurydice's direction I realised that she was already staring blatantly in mine. I looked down at my crotch frightened that I had begun to bleed again—but there was nothing, not even a stray pubic hair—before realising that it was my back that she was staring at and the circular scar in the shape of human teeth marks that decorated my left shoulder. I myself could not have seen it without a mirror but her gaze now became one for me. I was confronted by a dozen bruises, roses, caves, and open wounds, always bleeding.

Zeitgeist

I ran and jumped into the water. Then crouched down so that my whole body was submerged. I let my breath out very slowly and a stream of bubbles surged up to the surface while a shoal of fish surrounded my heels, feasting on the dead skin there before moving up towards the edges of the wrist-support and the rough places where it chafed. At first it tickled but then as I grew used to it and to the pressure of the water it was restful. I floated upwards. The cliffs above me formed a soft yet ragged circle and as I lay there staring into it sun spots danced over my eyes. I felt as if the whole scene glimmered and undulated with me. As if it were a part of my self, and as if this self then rippled out into the world. There was no one sick man of Europe only sick and sicker parts. Greece was the cliffs, the sky, a circle of human teeth marks, and the sun that burned itself into my retinas I thought dizzily, whereas England was an amputated or worse still phantom limb . . .

Surrounded

The only other swimmers were a red-faced German family of the type that looked extremely sturdy now but would at some point run to fat. I watched as the father raised their child, a little boy, onto his back and then began paddling in my direction. The mother who was standing on the other side of the lake bent down and dipped her head into the water, taking hold of her ponytail and coiling it slowly around the top of her head. Momentarily I considered the leftist, intellectual Greeks who viewed Brexit as a stand against the Germans, but then remembered Golden Dawn, the Fourth August Regime, and their admiration of Nazi aesthetics. So I switched to the Axis Occupation, the phrase 'If you want German efficiency, go to Switzerland,' and the concept of function-ware, but then remembered the brilliance of the Berlin Philharmonie. I tried to compare the Greek psyche to the German psyche, which was a bit like a more sensible version of the English psyche, and then Psyche to Cupid, and London's National Gallery to the Rijksmuseum in Amsterdam . . .

And then I ducked back underneath the water but rose immediately, gasping for breath. The German father and his son were coming nearer and seeing this I began to swim away with precise, even strokes. I circled the lake two, three, four times without stopping then let myself sink into the soft muddy grasses that fringed the sides. Clouds of brown rose up through the water that was no longer clear and the fish swarmed back. I let my body go limp and still, hoping that this would encourage them to eat me.

The Lyre of Orpheus

Hours passed before I hauled myself out of the water and put on one of the complimentary bathrobes. Then went over to the sun-lounger on which Eurydice was sleeping. Her breasts rose and fell in slight but heavy tremors. I noticed that she didn't shave her armpits and that there were faint black hairs at the corners of her mouth. I was still wet and as I continued to scrutinise her appearance a drop of water fell onto her forehead-

"Allegra?"

She raised herself up onto her elbows while I sat down beside her and picked up a towel.

I wrapped it around my head but not my face and said, "I want to know the myth of Eurydice."

She reached for her menthols. I could tell she was uncertain but also that as I was her guest she would probably indulge me. I waited while she took a drag then exhaled and as she did so the smoke rose like the mists of time between us.

"Well . . ." she began, and then, "Eurydice— the Eurydice—was the wife of Orpheus, a musician who was as famous for his charm as for his skill, and so of course many women wanted him. Yet it was Eurydice he loved, very deeply, and on their wedding day he played a song so beautiful that everyone who heard it wept with joy. Except Hymen, the marriage god. He didn't like Orpheus, or his playing, and so he made a terrible prophecy: that the union was doomed."

"Go on," I said in the voice of a housewife who only eats soft centres.

"Well, at first he and Eurydice were happy, until one day, Eurydice went out walking. Aristaeus, who was either a shepherd or a beekeeper-"

"But what's your fantasy?"

"My . . .?" For a moment she looked puzzled, and then "Oh, a beekeeper I suppose. So Aristaeus happened to be passing, and he took one look at Eurydice and decided that he had to have her, or to be precise that he was going to rape her. So of course Eurydice started to run. Only as she was running she stepped on a viper. It bit her and she died. Orpheus was distraught because-"

"He was going to fill all her holes?"

"Excuse me?" and although the towel had slipped slightly meaning that I was unable to see Eurydice's eyes I could tell by her tone that she had narrowed them, "Was she leaking?"

"I only meant that he wanted to complete her," I said meekly, "please, I'm listening, do go on."

"Well, as I said he was distraught. And so he wept, and played sad songs about how he, and not

Eurydice, should have died, and it was all so terribly sad and terribly beautiful that all the other gods wept too. And then eventually they decided that because Orpheus was so special and so talented they would grant a dispensation, and allow him to visit the underworld and retrieve his bride, except that there was one condition: he must walk in front of Eurydice and until they were both back in the upper-world he must not look back."

"But why?"

"Because it's a *story*," said Eurydice, with unexpected sharpness, and then without waiting for me to prompt her she continued, "So Orpheus went down to the underworld and found Eurydice. But because she had to walk behind him and he could not see or hear her he began to doubt that she was really there. As soon as he reached the daylight he looked back to check that she hadn't disappeared but because she had still to cross the threshold the agreement was broken, and Eurydice had to remain behind."

"But that's tragic," I said indignantly.

"Tragic shmagic," said Eurydice, and laughed.

She Who Widely Extends

I picked up another towel and wrapped it around my shoulders, feeling unexpectedly cold, while Eurydice stood up and walked towards the water. I repositioned myself on what had been her sun-lounger and without selecting any music plugged my headphones into my phone, only PING! - The_Saracens_79 was back and all the louder for being pumped straight into my ears.

I looked down to see *Are you alone?* illuminated in a grey backlit font. Then looked up to see the German family talking to one of the waiters. A black circle moved slowly round the lake that I assumed must be Eurydice drifting in and out the grasses. I pushed my headphones in as far as they could go and replied in the affirmative. Then-

PING! *I'm looking at your profile picture, but I'd like to look at something a little more revealing . . .*

Again I thought about the Axis Occupation. Then took a deep breath and googled a series of body parts using their vernacular as opposed to anatomical terms. An endless array of female orifices immediately covered the screen which, due to their size and dimensions, resembled an obscene collection of postage stamps. At first I scanned the squares looking for those belonging to redheaded women before realising that as most of the girls had shaved their cunts they only needed to be white. Eventually I settled on a blonde, twenty-something splayed against rose wallpaper; an aesthetic touch which, I now decided, suited my idea of Allemande. I beheaded it then attached it to my reply. I had just pressed send when Eurydice returned and sat back down beside me.

Panting heavily she said, "I forgot to tell you what it means."

I handed back one of her towels.

"What what means?"

"My name. It comes from Eurudike – meaning 'she who widely extends.' "

The Golden Hour

I didn't really feel like going out again but neither did I feel strong enough to risk the wrath of Ivan who had decided to 'treat me' to the opera. Somewhat dutifully I hung my swimming costume out to dry and changed into the gold dress and sandals that had now arrived courtesy of DHL. On the way out I paused and for the first time since I had arrived surveyed myself in the apartment's full length mirror. I was surprised to see that I looked much the same. Both those who did and did not know me would assume, correctly, that I had money. Also what those born into money regarded as good taste.

I ran the brush through my hair one final time, went outside and hailed a taxi. It took a little under an hour to reach the Cultural Centre which would have annoyed me further had I not already known that it would be an international crowd many of whom would appreciate my presence. As soon as I arrived I was surrounded by rich, dark-eyed women who over-spilled from heavy dresses that dripped with precious metal, and numerous dark-eyed men standing beside them, broad chested and impressive in matt black evening suits.

This, plus the excess of cigarette smoke created an effect akin to a dry-ice machine, lending the scene an aura of old-fashioned jet-set glamour in which, for a moment, I mistook Ivan's hazy figure for Dr. Agrios. Suddenly my desire for warmth, for human interaction, was so great that I actually ran towards him and-

"Dr. Agrios," I said, unable to stop myself from smiling.

"Who?"

"Sorry. No one. I . . ."

But on this occasion I let my sentence trail off into the sunset only because I knew that the sunset matched my clothes, and because some of the precious metals that adorned the other less talented women were the exact same colour as my hair. In the background I could see several members of the Athens Symphony Orchestra as well as Nigel Havers whom I had met at last year's Children-in-Need. We smiled and waved at one another.

κομψός

Ivan went to the bar and I turned my attention to an extremely elegant woman who was trying to buy a programme. She wore a beautiful shot silk tunic and matching hijab the top of which was decorated with a large emerald brooch. She was clearly very wealthy and

possibly important—for a second I wondered if she was Sheikha Mozah of Qatar—and yet the seller shook his head and told her in very sharp, very exact English that no more programmes were available.

The woman pointed to a pile of programmes stacked beneath the counter and in equally sharp, equally exact English enquired as to just who it was that this pile of programmes was intended for but instead of answering her the programme seller sucked his teeth.

I stepped forward not knowing quite what it was that I intended to do but before I could find out Ivan touched the back of my good hand. His flesh felt soft and comforting and once again and without meaning to I smiled.

A bell rang and the crowd began putting out their cigarettes. I picked up a glass of wine decanted into a plastic champagne flute. Then I took hold of Ivan's arm. Together we turned away and entered the auditorium.

The Dialogues of the Carmelites

The curtain lifted. I picked up the opera glasses and peered at the stage. The set was fashionably minimal. An array of monochrome cubes and spheres no doubt symbolising the various components of the nunnery— which would no doubt be reconfigured into different settings later on—were dotted across the floor and lit with a harsh blue light. For a long time there was silence. Then the beginnings of the music and the singers dressed in their black and white Carmelite habits moved in unison across the stage. Like the objects that constituted the set their bodies also cast long shadows so that, when stood in a group they resembled the trees in Eros' etchings.

The story centred on a young woman, Blanche, who had entered the nunnery in an attempt to escape the terrors of the French revolution. During the first act she sang about her struggle to comprehend violence, death, and the nature of faith. Then as the first and the second act progressed about how the faith that she had at first resisted gradually consumed her. By the third she had undertaken a vow of martyrdom and as the soldiers burst into the nunnery swore never to renounce her beliefs. The opera ended as the soldiers tore away her and the other nuns' veils, then forced them to ascend the guillotine, the blade literally cutting out their voices until only Blanche's remained, and her beautiful lyric soprano offered itself up to the God that she now loved.

I listened to her clear pure voice soaring upwards with the orchestra. I listened, without judging, to her and the orchestra and the clear pure sounds they made. I listened to the audience sigh, weep, and then applaud her. And then I listened to the silence that marked the space before the end. A pause, a pause, and then more clapping. And then the entire cast reappeared alive and wreathed in smiles.

The Opera

It was the second time in as many weeks that I had allowed the vocals to take precedence, and that both the words of the libretto and the development of it had moved me. But I wondered if this was due to what I was hearing or the way that I was hearing it; not as a performer or the critic of a rival performer but as a member of the audience who wanted only to be entertained. I could see that Nigel Havers was enjoying a bottle of Chardonnay at a neighbouring table and as I raised my own plastic flute towards my lips he caught my eye. I smiled and waved again and made a mental note to find out whether he actually knew Vangelis.

Then I turned to Ivan and said, "The thing that I will always remember about tonight is how ultimately Blanche not only recognised that she had faith and that this faith was her vocation but that once she understood it she could not denounce it."

"It sounds as though you really *felt* something Allegra."

In spite of myself I blushed. I had been so certain that what I said was profound, so swept up in my emotions that I had naively assumed Ivan would want to be profound also. Except that of course he had responded otherwise and already soured our exchange.

"Do you remember Hui Yin's performance?" he continued very smugly, "She wasn't moved by cheap sentimentality-"

"But you said that-"

"Which is why while you continue to wallow she will begin to excel-"

"But you-"

"I?"

"I . . ."

But the sun had now set and this time my sentence trailed off into the darkness. The sounds of a commotion rose from the back of the bar. The elegant woman reappeared, somehow strangely dishevelled. The emerald brooch was missing from her hijab and she was clutching the shot silk fabric to her throat. She cried and pointed at the programme seller who was shouting incomprehensibly, or so it seemed to me, in Greek. An imposing elderly gentleman motioned to the woman while two of the men who had been behind the bar manhandled the programme seller outside. Then the elderly gentleman led the woman outside too, while making apologetic gestures.

The Ambassadors

But in the morning it was cooler. A blacked out van and a group of riot police were positioned in front of the Indian Embassy opposite the Conservatoire. Two Greek soldiers clad in the official uniform—what looked like pleated mini-skirts and pointed clogs with pompoms on the toes—marched past them, and as the soldiers kicked their legs in time with one another the pompoms jiggled. The police ignored them in order to smoke cigarettes, and the passers-by ignored the police in order to photograph the soldiers.

I waited until there was a break in the traffic and then ran across the road. There was still one week left until the autumn term officially started and the grounds—which were vast and modernist in their design—were more or less empty. A few young women with the same thickset beauty as Eurydice loitered beneath the charred remains of what a few months previous would have still been nature. There was no reason for them to be there besides myself and consequently I hung back waiting until they finally got up, before then following at a little distance as they entered the building and walked down a long concrete corridor where the pipes were purposefully exposed. At the end was a huge hall with a sunken performance space in the centre. I could hear the low burr of nervous chatter and above it Ivan's old-testament voice thundering about how history remembered the victors. Yet as soon as I entered everyone stopped. There was silence and then a sudden flurry of activity as the entire room collectively realised who I was. One of the girls that I had followed turned round and squinted at me, confused, and then blushed deeply. One of the tutors rushed up and shook my hand quickly followed by his colleagues. Everyone appeared extremely eager to meet me while at the same time ignoring Ivan. I wondered if they knew how grateful their behaviour made me but at the same time hoped that they didn't.

The Metronome

The first student had chosen a piece originally written for the clarinet and at odds with the, for want of a better word, stringiness of the cello. And the way he played, with too much flair and too much movement, or alternatively the way he tried far too hard to impress, was also at odds with the work's intention and-

"Stop," said Ivan and of course he stopped, "you're over communicating. Consider what is meant by understatement."

The boy began again and despite his shaking hands showed some improvement. I made a point of congratulating him then waited for the next student who then walked nervously towards a metronome and set it in motion.

"Stop," said Ivan before she had even picked up her bow, "to be perfectly in time is to be without rhythm. I want to hear the music breathe."

She stopped the metronome and then once she started playing was really rather good. Ivan let her complete the piece without interruption and when she finished I applauded. There was silence as another similar looking girl took over only this time she was accompanied by a piano that she immediately began to compete with.

"Stop," said Ivan before she had had the chance to drown it out completely, "where is the piano supporting you? And where are you supporting it?" She tried again but it was the same as before. "Stop," said Ivan with more force than was necessary, "you are not paying enough attention to the score. Always ask yourself: how much freedom do I really have?"

The girl nodded, trembling, and then continued to make the same mistakes. Ivan did not stop her again, I assumed because there would have been no point, while I took the opportunity to check my emails. There was only one, somewhat surprisingly from Hale, which I deleted without reading, and then I shut my eyes. Despite not having to do or say anything the masterclass was draining. Each 'stop' made me relive my youth, which had always been inseparable from my parents and then Ivan's ceaseless critique of it, from practice and purges and pain-

"Ms Le Clef," said one of the students and I realised that the last piece of music had now come to an end, "we were hoping that we could persuade you to let us take you out for dinner? It would be so good to hear what you think too."

I took a breath then very carefully said, "Usually I'd love to. But unfortunately I'm on very strong painkillers for my- for my wrist. And I-"

"Allegra has no interest in other people," Ivan cut into me. "It is better that she goes home to wallow than bores you with her past. You would only discover her feet of clay and become as disillusioned as I am."

A Fantasy Piece

I left by the back door. Or rather, I left via the opposite side of the building to the one where Ivan was headed, and which, according to my only guidebook, meant that I was now facing the Archeological Site of Lykeion. Yet all I could see was what looked like an annex outside of which a dirty plastic chair had been placed and behind it a scrubby patch of grass and the remainder of wild poppies.

I walked around the annex. It backed onto a tiny church the scale of which resembled the funerary chapel. A large bell hung from one of the enclosing walls and through the empty space behind it I could see a flat brown rectangle of earth. Some sections were under glass boxes. Others had been staked out, then cordoned off with ropes. A priest replete with long beard and floor length robe walked up to the bell and rang it.

I walked towards him, and then followed after as he turned and went into the church. Inside the walls were smooth and matt with frescos I failed to comprehend. A wall of images, separating the sanctuary from the place where the congregation sat, twinkled with silver plate. The majority depicted the mother and child, the metal surround broken to reveal their painted hands and faces. Similar artworks had also been placed on wooden stands draped with fringed fabric around which metal holders filled with tall beeswax candles had been placed. Around half was burning.

Two Greek voices, a man and a woman's, resonated from behind the iconostasis. They talked without pause, their words continually overlapping with each other. I was sure that the man's voice belonged to the priest who had now disappeared while I pictured the woman as being of the same stout type as those that tended graves.

Then all of sudden the voices stopped. There was the sound of receding footsteps and then silence. I sat and listened to it. Then I reached for my phone and checked my messages. There was one from Albion who had obviously still not received my postcard. I tapped on it and read:

So?

Are you coming tomorrow or aren't you? And if so what time will you arrive?

You can't just leave me here trying to guess what you're planning. I'm not a mind reader.

Still Your Devoted Husband (whether you like it or not)

Albion

I sighed and then as my breath faded into the silence resumed listening to it. It was so cool and peaceful in the church that I was reluctant to leave. I closed my eyes and put my headphones in. Then I opened my eyes and PING! The_Saracens_79 now all too familiar, *Are you alone?* popped up on the screen. I removed my headphones, and strained to hear the sound of distant footsteps - but nothing. I waited for ten minutes but still none came. I waited for another five sighed again and typed, *No*. And then, without stopping:

> *Define romance*
> *Define a romantic moment*
> *Describe a romantic moment physically*
> *Describe a romantic moment mentally*
> *Describe a romantic moment that is also a sexual moment*
> *Describe a sexual moment that is also moment of realisation*
> *Define fear*
> *Tell me about your fears while growing up*
> *Tell me about fear of your mother*
> *Tell me about fear of your father*

Tell me about your favourite piece of art
Tell me about your favourite piece of music
What do you see when you look in the mirror?
What do you hear when something wonderful happens?

And then I pressed send. I neither wanted nor expected to hear from him again.

III

Reformation

The banner stated: *Making Music 8th September – 14th December, 2016* and underneath it a string quartet, sawing their way through Elgar; an imposing, inappropriately British, last-night-of-the-proms-nationalistic but at the same time peculiarly enjoyable choice. Each member of the quartet was a technically good-looking woman but in such a broad and well-scrubbed way that they had all rendered themselves quite sexless. Compared to the quartet or to any other person in attendance I appeared almost wanton but more because of my clothing's lack of practicality—again the gold dress and matching sandals—than its revealing nature.

I tried not to flinch as the cellist pressed her thumb, too hard, against the string, then took a glass of wine from one of the waitresses. Albion's eyes had a pink, dehydrated tinge and the buttons tugging around his stomach showed that he had put on weight – both things I hoped that the other women, stray interns in particular, might find off-putting . . .

"Mrs Le Clef-" began the Director.

"Allegra, please."

"Allegra."

He shook my bad hand then turned back to Albion. Suddenly I was overcome by the urge to reach out and stroke my husband's arm only of course I didn't. Because I didn't want to do anything that might reveal my doubts that he was mine. And then as if somehow sensing my desire the Director's wife touched me on the small of my back instead-

"Do you think that it's a case of nominative determinism?" and her tone implied that she was intending to be humorous, "Johannes and I are convinced that it must be."

"I'm not sure I understand?"

"Albion's surname. And yours too I imagine. Do you think that's why he knows so much about music?"

"I suppose so. Or what it looks like anyway."

Another waitress walked past holding another tray of drinks. The Director's wife deposited her empty glass on it and picked up a full one.

She took a sip and said, "But he knows so much about the cello. It was his idea to have the quartet."

"And Elgar?"

She looked confused.

I also took another sip and still smiling said, "The composer."

"Ah ha! Something tells me you're musical too?"

I looked back at Albion who was now talking to a girl who might have been me ten, fifteen, maybe even twenty years ago, or alternatively to Anker. Her red hair was tied in bunches and her cheeks were apple ripe. Whenever Albion said something laughter rippled through her and whenever she said something he beamed appreciatively.

I looked back at the Director's wife, still smiling, and then when I had just about got a handle on the situation said, "I am actually yes. In fact I play the cello."

"Oh? How interesting." She also looked at Albion then back at me again, "I always think it's terribly important to have one's own hobbies. Otherwise, well, resentments *can* build. Did you know that I run an interior design business?"

"Oh?" I echoed her, "How interesting."

"Yes, it's just a part-time thing, mainly advice on who to buy from, but still . . ." She took another sip of wine, "Do you give lessons?"

"I'm sorry?" Again, my gaze had been drawn back towards Albion and the girl, "I- the- the music. I didn't quite hear what you were saying."

"Do you give lessons?" the Director's wife repeated.

"Well funny you should ask. I just got back from teaching a masterclass. In Athens."

"Oh?" She clearly had no idea what a masterclass was but as I was still smiling she was still smiling also, "That sounds . . ."

"Interesting?"

169

"Oh yes it does," she drained the remainder of her drink then smiled again but this time with an air of gratitude that had not been there before, "Extremely."

"Oh yes it was. Extremely," and I drank and smiled also and then simply because I couldn't think of anything else to say said, "Young people are our future."

"Oh yes. We are always keen to attract young people."

She moved her arm as if to imply 'all this' and as I followed her gesture I once again saw Albion. And the girl who could have been me but better. And a thousand well-scrubbed giants towering over them, and yet despite their awful playing the beauty and the simplicity of the work shone through.

I looked back at the Director's wife and still smiling, just, said, "You know I'm ashamed to say I've not yet seen everything. But what you've done – all this," and now not just my words but my whole body echoed hers as I made the same movement with my arm, "would you mind if I . . . ?"

Making Music

I found a relatively quiet corner and also a leaflet. According to the introduction — which I could tell from the rhythm was not Albion's — the haphazard way in which I been approaching the work was wrong and there was actually a precise and particular order that each piece should be seen drawn-up in accordance with serious curatorial concerns. So I returned to what I now knew was the beginning and looked at a collection of antique instruments made from delftware and other pots in the shape of violins. Then I turned my attention to the selection of paintings that hung above them. Each one was old and figurative and meticulously realised in dark predominantly brownish colours. The accompanying wall texts, repeated in English, Dutch, German and French, read:

> "Perched atop the virginal, a keyboard instrument of the harpsichord family, is a monkey, who warns against the dangers of carnal desire."

> "The Lute player represents the sense of hearing. On the wall behind him hangs *The Deluge* – a warning that there is more to life than pure sensual pleasure."

> "The image can be interpreted as an admonition to praise God with singing and music-making, but also as a bawdy scene of seduction."

I wanted to spit out my wine but didn't dare to. Instead I went into the next room where copper wires were attached to concrete blocks. Cold, synthetic sounds resonated from them resulting in music—if it could be called that—with a distinctly purist bent. It was here that the comparatively younger people had gathered gulping down free booze. The girls had twisted their hair into topknots and wore crumpled asymmetric blouses. The boys had the same topknots and wore the same blouses bar one whose pink tee-shirt bore the words 'Gender Construct'. Looking at him, I thought of the hospital in Athens and what had once been my insides. I remembered how I had stood on the balcony screaming and the numerous holes that I had been born with as well as those that had been bored into me since. I wondered what sort of sound my cunt would make if someone put a copper wire inside it. I imagined something moist and unpleasant like a stagnant puddle – or else Verity shaking her flute . . .

Husbands and Wives

"Mrs Le Clef?"

I became aware that another tall blonde woman was standing beside me.

"Allegra, please."

"Allegra. Anya. The Head of Development's wife."

Another waitress walked past holding another tray of drinks and both Anya and I took one. Again we talked small talk and then when there was nothing more to be wrung out we expressed our sorrow at having to be elsewhere.

I was about to pick up another leaflet only before I could do so a different, deeper voice said, "Mrs Le-"

"Allegra!" but then I laughed as if I had been joking, "I mean please. There really is no need for everyone to be so formal."

"Of course. Allegra. Jan, Annika's husband."

I smiled very brightly and began to repeat the same small fragments of my life and as I did so it occurred to me firstly that I still did not know the name of the Director's wife and secondly that it would be far too awkward to try and ascertain it now-

"I don't suppose you really need to though," said Jan.

"I'm sorry?" Again, I had allowed my thoughts to wander, "I- the- the installation. I didn't quite hear what you were saying."

"I don't suppose you really need to though," Jan repeated. "Obviously you have to understand what music means to other people, to those who made the paintings or . . ." He looked in the direction of the concrete blocks, "Or installations. But Mr Le Clef, Albion, it's his job to think in pictures not in sounds."

Another waitress with another tray of drinks walked past.

"But he knows so much about the cello."

"Oh . . . ?"

But I had nothing more to add. Both Jan and I expressed our sorrow at having to be elsewhere. I picked up another leaflet and continued on my way. I drifted through clusters of small crackle coated paintings and large explosive sculptures. Through warm white wine and cold post-modern shrieks. Through middle-aged couples in hard expensive lines and twenty-something gender-neutrals. And then I was back where I had started. Beside Albion who was surrounded by women while I waited on the fringes, alone.

Too Hard

I made my way towards the string quartet then bent down so that my mouth was level with the cellist's ear and said, "Stop. You're pressing too hard. Remember, playing is about motion, not pressure."

She nodded nervously but showed a small improvement. I smiled encouragingly then closed my eyes and let the music swirl around me almost forgetting I was there. When I finally opened them again I realised that Mariella Frostrup was waving at me. I waved back, and made a mental note to say 'hello' before the evening ended. Then I took out my phone. There were no new or unread messages but I tapped the screen anyway and as if replying to something urgent.

Un-Framing

The Dinner that then followed was interminable. A tangle of never ending pleasantries. Earnest but always positive appraisals of the art. Earnest and always negative critiques of the political ideologies that financed the aesthetic ideologies that critiqued them. And then more of it. My position within the world of classical music had been far simpler in that all the grubby sucking-up had been left to other people. And because I had automatically been at the experience's centre I had never really had to try.

"What we have to ask ourselves," said the Director to Albion, "is just what it is that this un-framing frames?"

"Or alternatively," said Albion to the Director, "whether or not the un-framing is in itself a performative act?"

"Eventually I hired someone else to run the social media account," said the Director's wife to the Head of Development's wife, "I tell her how I feel about the space and she finds coordinating cushions."

"Oh? How interesting,' said the Head of Development's wife.

"Oh yes very," said the Head of Development.

I looked round the table for the younger redhead but she had gone. I tried to remember the name of the Director's wife but couldn't. I felt cast-out, absent, somewhere else-

"Do you like Rossetti?" I said, grabbing the arm of the Waitress who had just walked by with a fresh bottle of prosecco, "I've always felt that, had I lived at another time I could have been his muse. Albion used to have one of his portraits hanging in the study, but then one day jealousy overcame me and I slashed her in the face."

I had intended to come across as darkly humorous but could tell from the Waitress' expression that my behaviour seemed unhinged. The Director's wife remained blissfully unaware however, which in turn confirmed that she had not been listening to anything that I had said.

"And do you know Amsterdam at all, Allegra?" the Director's wife continued turning towards me as she took the bottle of prosecco from the Waitress and topped up our both glasses. "I could arrange a tour if you'd like, perhaps with one of the interns?"

"Oh? How interesting . . ."

And once more I became an echo, while at the same time picturing the sharp edge of a bronze paperweight tearing into what should have been a nose.

Leftovers

Afterwards I fell asleep immediately, and then when I woke many hours later the space next to me was cold. There was also a feeling of dampness, spreading. I reached down and gingerly touched the crotch of my knickers, which were soaked in blood. Then drew back the sheet and saw the extent of the stain that was seeping out across the gold silk dress and onto the white cotton beneath it.

I removed my clothes, stripped the bed and went into the kitchen where I buried everything at the bottom of the recycling bin. As an afterthought I also added the gold sandals on the grounds that they no longer had a dress to match them. Then I went into the bathroom and turned on the shower. The water was too hot but I made it hotter still—so that even the steam was burning—and scrubbed my skin until it was raw. I looked down and saw that my pubic hair was caked in a deep fleshy something. I kept on looking at it and all the while I thought about how strange it was that I could keep on bleeding but still not die.

I dried myself and put on a clean pair of knickers that I then stuffed with balls of rolled up toilet paper. Then I went into the living room opened my laptop and logged onto my email. I had three new messages: one from the record company entitled 'Final Cover,' one from the British Council entitled 'Many Thanks,' and one from Anker De Jong entitled 'Canal Houses.' "

I went back into the kitchen but when I looked behind me I saw that I had left a trail of blood upon the floor. There was a sponge lying next to the sink. I picked it up and half-heartedly wiped the floor, spreading the mess in a watery swirl. I opened the fridge and after a brief survey of its contents removed a piece of steak. I laid it on the worktop, went through the kitchen drawers until I found a rolling pin then hit the flesh until it was tender.

I cooked the steak in butter and even though it was not yet eleven poured myself a glass of merlot. I ate and drank without stopping and as soon as I had finished poured myself a second glass of wine. Then I stuck my fingers down my throat and vomited over the sink before rinsing both it and my mouth with lime-cordial.

I didn't want to call Albion because Albion already knew too much about the filth of my insides but I knew too that I needed to see a doctor. I went back into the living room and picked up his other phone. I scrolled through the contacts until I came to 'Shithead's Wife'. I pressed call. It went straight to voicemail.

I took a deep breath and in my lightest voice said, "Hello, this is Albion's wife, Allegra. I wanted to call and say thank you for hosting such a very lovely and also very interesting evening, oh and for arranging the tour of the canal houses. Anker—you've got a real star there—well, she just emailed me. Oh, and if you've got a moment, could you also pass on the name of a doctor? Women's troubles, ha ha. I don't seem to have one and it really would be very much appreciated. You can reach me on plus-four-four . . ."

The Doll

An hour later I was at the Doctor's surgery, a colourful establishment filled with modular furniture. The Receptionist greeted me in English and gestured towards a chair that appeared to have been designed solely to assist one's posture. I sat down, feeling my spine straighten as I did so, but also fearing that I must now appear to be ridiculously self-important. Fortunately the only other patients were a woman of around my age who was preoccupied with a magazine and a little girl, presumably her daughter, who played on the floor by her feet. The little girl was holding a doll with a round black hole in the middle of its mouth into which she pushed a bottle filled with water. After a while the water began to drip out of the doll's bottom. The little girl giggled delightedly and then proceeded to tie her mother's scarf around its legs in an approximation of a nappy.

When she had finished she held it out towards me and said, "Vind je mijn schat leuk?"

I tried to smile.

"Yes, very nice."

The mother looked up from her magazine.

"I'm sorry," she said in a soft strained voice, and then in a harder one "Mia! Kom hier!"

I thought it amusing that 'Mia! Come here!' in Dutch sounded like 'Mia! Come here!' in English if one said it with a funny Dutch accent and then that everything everywhere must sound like this to someone somewhere else. I loved the sound of my cello because it sounded like Albion's professional voice. Or alternatively, I loved the sound of what could have been another sound because I preferred my experiences to be mediated either though music, images, or pain. I too was a leaking doll I thought ruefully—something that sounded funny in any language—because I was, essentially, an English construct and not always so easy to translate.

Fuge

"Ms Le Clef?" said the Receptionist, "The Doctor will see you now."

I got down from my orthopaedic throne and entered a smaller, cosier version of the waiting room. All the wood was a light untreated pine and a man with similar colouring was sitting on another, very functional chair.

He looked up from his notepad and in a voice that was entirely devoid of either charm or emotion said, "Ms Le Clef."

"Yes."

"So, I see that you recently had an abortion-"

"It wasn't an abortion," I cut in.

"Okay. But nonetheless you were given abortion medication?"

"I . . ."

"And that was in Athens?"

"Yes."

I looked at the yucca plants lined up on the window sill and then out through the window behind them. Each of my previous abortions—three in all—had taken place in the very early stages. They had been quick and painless lunchtime appointments without the need for surgery. I hadn't dwelt on them afterwards just as I hadn't dwelt on smear tests or dental hygiene appointments, which by and large had been more intrusive. Yet the Borders Incident as I now mentally dubbed it was unlike the others in that, on this last occasion it was not I who had attempted to evict my uninvited guest but rather the guest in question who had turned on me. And then turned to stone. A stone that then hung like a dead weight around my neck reminding me that my fertility—the one possible alternative to my sickness—was decreasing . . .

"Okay," said the Doctor.

He reached inside his desk and took out a sheet of paper—a multiple choice questionnaire—which he then handed to me along with a retractable pencil. The questionnaire referred to length, quantity, and type of blood loss, as well as other symptoms such as dizziness and vomiting. Usually each question had four possible answers labelled 'a,' 'b,' 'c,' and 'd'. Occasionally the possible answers took the form of black and white diagrams. The retractable pencil was the kind that architects used and made sharp, staccato clicks.

"Now if you could fill that in for me?" said the Doctor.

I nodded and let my good hand move quickly, expertly, across the paper circling the relevant letters as though they were musical notes. I handed it back and resumed looking out of the window—the view was, perhaps unsurprisingly, of a canal—while the Doctor cast his eye over my responses.

After a moment he said, "Well I don't think that, at this stage, there's too much to worry about. But we do need to consider certain lifestyle factors-"

"But I did do some volunteering," I said plaintively, "at a refugee centre. And while I admit that I could have- should have done more I-"

"What about exercise?"

"Oh I see what you mean."

"Because a heavy workload, or even something as basic as a lack of sleep, all of these things put stress upon the body, which in turn delays the healing process. And what about your diet? For example caffeine, and refined sugars-"

"I had steak for breakfast," I cut in again and then, wanting to make myself sound less weird, "for the iron content," and then wanting simply to be better and alone, "but couldn't I just have some antibiotics? Please?"

"Ms Le Clef," and the Doctor's voice took on the same hard tone as the woman in the waiting room's had when admonishing her daughter. "That really isn't something that I'd feel comfortable prescribing."

Anker

"Allegra?"

"Normally people call me Mrs Le Clef."

"You would prefer me to call you Mrs Le Clef?"

"No, no of course not," I said irritably, "Allegra's fine."

After the doctor's appointment I had returned to Albion's apartment, gone to bed again, woken up again, felt wretched again – almost as if I was still in Blighty – and now here I was waiting again, although this time it was for the Valkyrie who seconds earlier had been hurtling towards me to finish locking her bicycle to the railings.

Yet this woman that I was now almost face to face with was not the pretty redhead from the exhibition private view but an incredibly tall blonde with the same broad, well-scrubbed appearance, and the same indomitable aura of practicality that all the Dutch appeared to possess.

I relaxed, slightly, and turned my attention to the Concertgebouw on the opposite side of the Museumplein. I remembered the last time that I had played there and the numerous accolades that I had received and in this one brief, moment of remembering that was also forgetting I was suddenly sure my talent couldn't have really left me, and so much so that it was almost as if I could feel the bone in my wrist growing back . . .

". . . So would you rather walk or hire a bicycle?" said Anker.

"I'm sorry?" and I tried to pay attention, "I- the- the music . . ."

"The music?"

"I'm sorry, I didn't quite hear what you were saying."

"Would you rather walk or hire a bicycle?" Anker repeated.

"Oh . . ." I pointed to my wrist, "I'm still not meant to put any weight on it, So . . ."

"Of course," said Anker, but without any of the awkwardness that such references to my body more usually provoked, and then clearly noting how I kept on looking behind me, "You already know a little of the city?"

"Well . . ." I began, as Anker led me off in another direction and the Concertgebouw slowly disappeared from view, "Well I . . ."

PING! went a bicycle bell.

PING! went my phone.

I reached inside my bag.

"You would like to talk on your phone? Or to answer my question?" said Anker, matter-of-factly.

"Oh, well I'll . . . I mean I . . ."

I took out my phone, tapped the message and read: *Johnnie and I arrive tomorrow. Apparently, Holland is a wealthy country, with lots of lovely tulips. Expecting you and A to entertain us, S X.* Then, re-read it two more times while laughing, inwardly, at the silly provocative space that lay between the initial and the kiss as well as the fact that she and that ridiculous man were still together and, presumably, in love. Suddenly I felt light, frivolous, and no longer frightened by discussions that would no longer have space to occur. I re-read the message a third time and without intending to I laughed out loud.

"Good news?" said Anker.

"Oh, it's just a friend of mine. She and her partner are coming to visit me- I mean us, while we're here. She's very . . . gregarious."

"How nice!" exclaimed Anker continuing to march briskly forward, "Now Albion has not just you but all your friends to entertain him!"

Prokofiev

The words, 'Andreas Post – dealer of fine violins, violas, cellos, bows. Expertises – Valuations – Restoration – New Instruments' were written in large gold letters above us. Yet the window underneath them was completely empty so that one could see right inside and the cases lined up against the shop's back wall. When viewed altogether they were as dense and foreboding as Cyprus trees or Carmelite nuns or . . . *cellos,* and when I looked at them I shivered . . .

"Are you unwell?" said Anker.

"Oh no, honestly, I'm fine," and I made an effort to stand up straight, "I- I was just wondering if there was a Montagnana. That's the one I play."

Anker took off her rucksack and pulled out a sparkly purple scarf. It was so awful that it reminded me of Verity - as well as how she hadn't been in touch.

"I'm afraid I only know about electronic music. With the classical stuff I just wouldn't know where to start," said Anker.

"Prokofiev," I said meanly.

"Prokofiev?"

She took out her phone and googled 'Prokofiev cello' then plugged her headphones in. As we resumed walking her expression grew increasingly confused, first as the result of what I assumed was the music, squirming inside her ears, and then a crowd of British men who ran past us with a blow-up doll.

"It's a struggle," she said, amiably and put the headphones back inside her pocket, "and although we Dutch acknowledge man's depravity we prefer not to dwell on it."

Gezelligheid

Despite myself I laughed again. Because despite myself both Anker and the ridiculous picture book houses that now rose up around us were charming. Without saying anything I stopped and entered the café on our right. Through the window I could see that the British men were now running back the other way and that the blow-up doll had a puncture. I ordered two takeaway coffees, paid for them, and said, 'thank you,' in English to the English barista. Then I went back outside and-

PING! went a bicycle bell.

PING! PING! PING! went three more beside them.

"I think I'd find it hard to live so close to other people," I said, trying not to spill either mine or Anker's coffee as one of the cyclists grazed my shoulder, "I couldn't bear everyone knowing my business."

"That's why there is no English word for gezelligheid."

"An err, a gazelle- a what?"

"Gezelligheid. It's Dutch way of living together, or on top of each other. It's the difference between saying 'What will the neighbours think?' and 'Think of the neighbours.' "

PING!

Another cyclist went by but this time with a violin case covered in scuffs and stickers strapped to his back. I assumed that he must be a busker with the 'expertises' of a performing monkey, then thought of Verity again, and how she still hadn't called me. I scrunched my empty coffee cup into a crumpled ball and not caring who saw or disapproved threw it in the water-

"I think it's best just to avoid the neighbours altogether," I said, failing to keep the anger from my voice.

Our Lord in the Attic

Anker placed her larger hand upon my smaller arm and I realised that we had reached our destination. She had emailed me an extensive list of canal houses but I had barely glanced at it preferring to fill my time with worthy—neigh saintly—occupations such as bleeding. Consequently I no idea what the reception led to but simply followed Anker through it and down a rickety flight of steps at the bottom of which was an old-fashioned kitchen. The walls were covered in blue and white tiles and the few pieces of wooden furniture contained therein – a chair, a table, a dresser – had all been painted in the same matt yellow. There was also a hearth with pans hanging over it and, somewhere behind a curtain, what I took to be a primitive toilet.

"It's very . . . authentic," I said uncertainly.

Anker nodded. She seemed strangely at home in this too old-fashioned, too wholesome space and for a second I thought I saw a row of rainbow socks hung up to dry beside the fire. I blinked then took a photo of the blue and white tiles, tilting my head to one side in a way that I hoped would pass for interested. Anker waited for me to finish and then when finally convinced that I had had enough she led the way up a second staircase that was situated at the room's far end.

This time we emerged in the middle of a hall. A large but very simple candelabra hung in the centre of the ceiling. Several small oil paintings, landscapes mainly, had been placed at regular intervals along the walls alongside the now standard blue and white pottery. Everything I saw made me think of *Making Music,* and how it had decried any form of pleasure. Everything was so protestant, so smug and happy in its own denial. I looked at the stiff, murky trees that marked the landscapes and thought of the dour, pinch-lipped people who waited, eternally, for *The Deluge.* Everything felt stale and ugly and above all silent.

"It's very authentic," I repeated.

No. 1 in G major, K. 313

Yet the final room into which Anker now showed me appeared to belong to a completely different time or even country. The floor, which ran the length of the entire building, was covered in a plain rush matting and the walls, which turned into a double, maybe even triple, height vaulted ceiling were painted titanium white. But this was relieved firstly by the weird mauve panelling of the gallery above, and secondly by the huge Baroque alter. Clouds and cherubs of a very loose and fleshy type floated over it alongside a dozen other mournful and sensuous statues made from painted plaster, marble scrolls with purple veins, and rose pink marble pillars. In my mind's ear I could hear *Mozart's Flute Concerto*—one of Verity's favourite pieces—the lightness and unreality of which overwhelmed me. At the same time I knew that these statues and others like them cried tears of blood and lived their lives—be they on earth or elsewhere—with their wounds forever open.

"I- I- don't understand," I said, because we could have been in France or Italy or some other magical, gilt-edged dream place, and because a flute was playing, soaring, tripping inside me in such a pretty feminine voice that in this one, unique moment it was even sweeter to me than the rich tenor of my cello-

"That the Netherlands is a tolerant place?"

"But . . ."

But Anker who was clearly enjoying my reaction simply took off her scarf and shoved the entire thing inside her rucksack so that it would almost certainly be crumpled later on.

"But . . ." I began again, and then more forcefully, "but why is all this" and I moved my arm so that without meaning to I made the same expansive gesture as the Director's wife had, "here?"

"Well, because the man who built this house was a man who thought of his protestant neighbours, and so his neighbours, who appreciated his discretion, didn't try and pry inside his catholic heart."

"An example of gazelle err, gazelle . . . that gazelle thing."

"Yes!" and her wholesome, open face beamed down upon me so clearly pleased that I had finally succumbed to this more tactful, practical and thus superior way of thinking, "He was gezelling!"

"No," and the panic was back boiling acid in my stomach. "No, he was dishonest. And he should have been punished. Severely."

Unruly

I went to bed again, alone again, at seven-thirty then woke to see morning light through the gap beneath the curtains. I kept my breathing slow however and only when the sound of the shower hissing told me that it was safe to do so fully opened my eyes. Then I reached for my laptop, logged onto my email and stared unblinkingly at it, and after an indefinite amount of time had passed slowly typed the following:

Dear Verity,

As you are aware, I have not been well. Nevertheless, I know how much Pilates means to you and understand why you felt the need to prioritise a yoga retreat over the wellbeing of your oldest and closest friend . . .

"Allegra, what are you doing?"

I let my finger drop and then relax upon the backspace key in a manner reminiscent of Casals and then watched as my aggression recoiled back into the illuminated page.

Then I pulled the collar of my flannelette pyjamas up around my neck, and still staring at the white-washed screen said, "Emailing Verity. I thought seeing as Scarlett and Johnnie were visiting she might as well come too."

"The point being?"

"The point being fun."

Albion came back into the bedroom and picked up his clothes. As he reached down the towel that had been wrapped around his waist dropped onto the floor. Suddenly his penis like all penises struck me as obscene. I thought of Athens' fallen rich and the wealthy, uptight protestants who funded the Museum's conceits. I thought of heaven or some other style of void. And then of my wedding dress that was as soft as swansdown and matched my hidden throat . . .

I shut my eyes and in as light a voice as possible said, "Now you'll have not just me but all our friends to entertain you."

"Allegra. Allegra *please*."

192

The white noise rose inside my ears but I resisted the urge to stick my fingers into them and instead said, "The truth is. I've always been afraid of grovelling at your feet."

"What?"

"Nothing."

"But Allegra-"

"It's nothing!"

Dear Verity,

I hope that you enjoyed your retreat. Scarlett and Johnnie are coming to stay and I wondered if you would like to join us? The Dutch are 'erg sportief,' and most restaurants now offer a vegetarian option . . .

My hair, my skin, my mouth were dry. I picked up the glass of water sitting on the bedside table and drank some of it. Gradually the buzzing dropped.

I waited until it had died away completely and then said, "Anyway, you don't need to worry. Verity will find a health-conscious excuse."

Albion laughed.

"Verity will relax once she's pregnant."

"Pregnant?"

"That's what's behind the fads isn't it?"

"Oh, I never thought- I mean- I . . ."

"But I don't want to talk about Verity. I want to talk about us."

I looked down at my long white fingers. They reminded me of a painting of hands or a painting of a painting of hands or the hands that a swan would have had had swans had hands . . . I thought that they were beautiful but that they didn't work. And then that they were pointless. Again the backspace key. Again a small erasure-

Dear Verity . . .

"So why are you here, Allegra?"

"Me?"

"Who else? Who else is here?"

"Well, I know that you are, but I . . ."

I looked at my hands, then felt the bedding move as Albion sat down beside me. His shoulders were bent and his head was lowered so that it almost touched his knees.

I looked at the back of his head and said, "Albion, please, I don't expect you to- to understand, but . . ."

But my body remained unsupervised and therefore unruly. It held its good hand up in so that its index finger obscured the first word on the screen and Verity was no longer dear but a singular, solitary fact. When set in relief against the bright white laptop its skin resembled unclean sheets. Its fingers were thinner than they had been and the gold ring was becoming loose . . .

"If you don't want me then why are you here?"

My body turned its hand this way and then that. Its cuticles were ragged and there was a sunspot on the back.

I took a deep breath and said, "I want to be with you but I . . ."

Finally Albion turned to face me, then shook his still wet head. Drops of water splashed onto and then ran down my cheeks. I considered getting out of bed and prostrating myself on the patch of parquet flooring that lay between the valance and the rug. I considered screaming, crying: *But I'm a cripple, you pervert, I'm a cripple!* But instead I pictured a paper bag expanding.

When I was almost calm I whispered, "I want to be with you, but I . . ."

"Yes?"

"But I'm a- I'm a . . ."

Pachebel's Canon

Albion laid his hand upon my arm. It made a damp patch on my flannelette pyjamas that from a distance could have been a stain. I knew that if I didn't reach out too, then the moment would be lost, but before my thoughts could turn to action the harpsichord and then the strings began to play. The music grew rapidly in volume and insistence and as it did the word 'Shithead' lit up Albion's phone. Straight away, he pressed answer. The music stopped, he stood up and began muttering into his sleeve. I went back to the laptop. This time I held up my other hand and positioned it in such a way that only the 'Dear' was visible. I pictured an epitaph written in Cyrillic and the wealthy, two-faced Catholics who had paid to hide their faith. I pictured heaven or some other style of nothing. And then my wedding dress that was as white as any new technology and matched my impression of what had once been hands . . .

"I'm sorry I have to go," said Albion.

I nodded at the screen. Albion found and then put on his jacket. I took another sip of water. Albion kissed me on the forehead. I nodded at the screen.

I miss you . . .

"But we'll talk more later?"

"Oh, but I . . ."

"Tonight? We'll talk?"

And again I wanted to agree only 'we' like 'us' had now become a concept in which I who was no one struggled to believe. I looked down at my ragged cuticles and too loose ring. I inhaled the stench of unwashed sheets. I relived my body crashing through the windshield and my wrist crumpling against the

196

metal bonnet. I considered getting out of bed and shitting on the patch of parquet flooring that lay between the valance and the rug-

"Yes, yes of course."

Albion picked up his wallet. I took another sip of water. Albion picked up his keys then headed towards the door-

Oh. Dear. Verity . . .

The door slammed shut. I considered slashing my stomach open and trying to find a stone.

Instead I spat at the laptop and said, "Kos omak!"

An indefinite amount of time passed. I let my finger glide across the backspace key in a manner reminiscent of Rostropovich then watched as the globule of saliva slid across the screen. I saw my shattered bones fizzing with the white noise of electrodes and a swan caught in a barbed wire fence.

Zuiderbad

But then I got up. Drank a vegetable juice. Followed by another probiotic drink. I attempted to get through to Verity. Failed. Attempted to get through to Hale. Failed. Attempted to get through to Scarlett. Succeeded.

Tried to make her complain about Verity. Failed. Threw the phone across the floor . . .

I bundled my swimming things into a bag and ran out of the apartment. I knew that there was a pool nearby, and that due to the climate—literal and otherwise—the journey there would be smooth yet unhurried. I jumped on a tram and ten minutes later I was there. None of the staff appeared to care about whether I had verrucas only whether I preferred to use one of the old-fashioned changing booths or the digitalised lockers. I opted for the former, put on my swimming costume and—overcome with a sudden, random sense of jubilation—leapt into the water, before realising that it was filled with kids.

At first I tried to weave between them but their splashing made it impossible to complete even a single length. I swam more aggressively, my arms slicing into them and yet they still refused to move. After a while I gave up and floated by the small tiled enclave at the pool's far end. A large fountain designed to resemble a miniature waterfall spouted from it. I leaned in so that it massaged my neck and shoulders. I thought about how picturesque I must have looked within this steamy soft-focus setting and then of Rossetti's *Water Willow*, which had always been one Albion and my favourites . . .

"You should try the herbal baths," said an English woman's voice.

I turned towards it and saw someone who going by her swimwear belonged to a similar social demographic as myself. I nodded politely and immediately looked up at the ceiling where a series of large metal beams cut across the wooden slats. I waited for a minute or so and then when I was sure that any possibility of a conversation had passed looked back out across the water. The lifeguard was talking to a boy poised half-way up the highest diving board's ladder. It was too far away to hear what the lifeguard was saying but it was clear from his expression that he was annoyed.

The woman beside me followed my gaze then raised her voice and shouted, "Marcus, get down from there!" and then, "I SAID GET DOWN FROM THERE RIGHT NOW!"

She and the lifeguard exchanged awkward smiles and the boy climbed down and wriggled back into the water. A younger child who had been waiting behind him watched silently and a second later followed suit.

"And look after your brother! He's only little!" and then, "HE'S LITTLE!"

The boys swam off and became lost amongst the churning throng while the woman beside me sighed.

Then realising that I had heard her sigh she laughed, turned back to me and said, "Normally I'd be the one in the herbal baths, but you know how it is - school holidays."

"Oh, of course," and the situation now began to make sense. "I was wondering why there were so many of them."

"You don't have any?"

"No."

"Lucky you." She laughed again. "It's only a matter of time before they rise up and kill us all with teaspoons!"

I laughed too, but uneasily, then tried to recall other nineteenth-century paintings that could fit the now current situation. The only one that I could think of was *The Triumph of the Innocents*; a grotesque depiction of the infant Jesus surrounded by martyred babies' ghosts. Each ghost was painted in strange pearlescent colours and each had an eerie bubble type structure attached to the top of its head. I had never understood the reason for the bubbles just as I had never understood exactly what it was that they, the murder victims, were supposed to have triumphed over before concluding that, unlike music, the visual arts only ever pretended to make sense.

Rossetti

I went in search of the herbal baths which, or so I now discovered, was actually a row of Jacuzzis with leaves and petals swirling in the water. Yet their location on a mezzanine behind the fountain was comparatively quiet. I could still see into the pool proper although at the same time I myself was obscured from view, a position that very much suited me.

I got in to the nearest empty bath and the water surged around my thighs like tiny rapids. I felt faint but not unpleasantly so. Rather it was as though I was floating in a sack of amniotic fluid completely safe and apart from the rest of the world. I shut my eyes and let myself sink slowly. Everything felt golden—more golden even than Greece—and this time it was Rossetti's *Beata Beatrix* that sprang to mind . . .

I shifted slightly and a stream of water pressed against my clitoris. Despite the complexities—or death —of my sex life masturbation had always struck me as straightforward. When I lost my virginity to Sebastian, I did so without loosing any blood. Initially I put this down to his technique of very slight jiggling, but in retrospect I had decided that it was because my girlhood's passing was not something that I mourned. The sex that had then proceeded this not-so-monumental event had been much the same, and after I had become bored of lying awake unsatisfied while at the same time not daring to voice my true desires I took to silently fingering myself beneath the sheets. The situation with Conrad-Boy had been similarly unrewarding although in this instance it was directly related to his alcoholism, and his failure to maintain an erection when drunk. Yet even after I had met Albion I continued to touch myself just as frequently, and always while remembering the last time that we had had sex. I had often wondered why this was and had almost come to the conclusion that it was only through remembering the moment that I could ever truly become part of it . . .

I closed my eyes, placed my hands across my ears and waited, but the scent of some indistinguishable essential oil made me think of Verity. I breathed out, only not one of my unwanted thoughts would leave. Gradually the thing that had been rising inside me faded and as I let my hands drop the noise of the children screaming filled my ears. I thought of Beata Beatrix massacred by the Innocents then pictured myself imprisoned in a pearlescent bubble. I wondered what I had done to make Verity not want to call me and why I kept on bleeding even though I was a ghost.

Café Rembrandt

Afterwards I caught another tram to the Museum, and then after Albion reprimanded me for my wet hair we took a taxi to the airport. The driver's presence ensured that there was little conversation while in the car, but our joint fear of being late meant that we arrived with more than an hour to be alone in. Having no need of either sunglasses or perfume we avoided the shops and instead found a cafe the location of which I then texted to Scarlett. Although the red, floor-to-ceiling curtains created a typical sense of northern European warmth my overall impression was that it was a little too like an

English pub and therefore not the type of place I usually frequented. I sat down in one of the quieter corners while Albion went over to the bar before returning a few minutes later with a plate of white bread sandwiches; items that served only to reinforce this, my initial impression. I picked one up and tore it into several sections then rearranged them so that, to the casual observer, it would be almost impossible to determine quite how little or how much remained.

"You must eat," said Albion, watching me.

"I ate a lot in Athens."

"But you're not in Athens anymore."

Or Kansas or London or anywhere else where I knew how to orientate myself, but at the same time I put a small piece of bread in my mouth.

I swallowed it and said, "I forgot to tell you. Yesterday I met up with Anker."

"Oh yes?"

"And I decided that she was a threat and not a promise."

Albion laughed. I picked up another piece of bread and then when he wasn't looking dropped it on the floor.

"Whereas the girl at the opening . . .?"

"Is the Director's daughter."

He laughed again and this time I joined in with him. I knew full well that sleeping with the Director's daughter would have created the type of complication he abhorred and that even though he also abhorred the

Director his preferred line of attack had always been to be beyond reproach. I looked down at the floor where my latest deceit lay like snow upon the ground. The word that came to mind was 'crumbs'.

"I hope that Johnnie isn't too annoying," I said feebly, "or that he looses his voice."

"I just hope that they don't want to do anything too extravagant," said Albion, biting into one of the sandwiches, "I haven't signed my next contract yet and, well you know . . ."

I assumed that he meant now that I wasn't working. Had he said this directly then I could have responded that the yet-to-be-released *Essential Le Clef* was expected to do well and that each of my previous albums still provided us with substantial royalties, but we had never been direct outside the bedroom and we were too old and too used to being us to start to do so now-

"But I caught a tram to the Museum," I said instead, "you were the one who insisted on a taxi."

"What I meant was that I don't like to feel indebted. You of all people should understand that."

And in response I didn't even bother to say, 'I.'

Because he was right. Both in that I didn't care to be on the receiving end of any uneven kindnesses— or demands to accept one's need for them—and in that he knew each of us well enough to know that we were indeed alike in that respect. Familiarity now tinged with intimacy began closing in around us but once again the outside broke us up before the moment could take root. There was a loud irreverent giggle, the red curtains parted, and Scarlett and Johnnie tumbled through them-

"Johnnie was just saying that he wants to see a peep-show!" screeched Scarlett before either Albion or I had had chance to even say, 'hello' to her, "He thinks that in our fully frontal modern world a little stealth will be good for our souls."

International Women of Mystery

But they were our guests, which meant that half an hour later we were in the centre of the red light district, which was the centre of the tourist district also. Each street was filled with kiosks selling bongs and key-rings shaped like ganja leaves and sex shops with the doors and windows painted black. In between them brothels opened out onto the street; rows of individual cubicles framed by red velvet curtains not dissimilar to those in the cafe and lit by overhead red lights.

The women who sat inside them wore only their underwear that did little to conceal their very ordinary bodies and I couldn't help but stare at them as Scarlett and I walked past. The women answered us with cold contemptuous looks whereas whenever Albion and Johnnie, who were already a few steps ahead, went by they tapped the glass and pouted. Watching them I wondered which was worse: sex with strange men or the strange women who judged you for it? And then I noticed how the leaves that were beginning to fall resembled rubies glimmering like sunken treasure in the middle of the water-

"Is that what you get up to in Harley Street then?" said Albion

"What- I'm sorry. The err . . ."

I looked where he was pointing, which was at a building signed the Hospital Bar. It was covered in a poorly airbrushed scene that depicted two young female nurses fondling each other's breasts while an elderly male doctor replete with white coat and stethoscope took notes. 'Real Fucking, Live Show' was written next to it in neon, and then repeated in English, Dutch, German and French - just like the Museum texts.

"You know I have been feeling a little under the weather," said Scarlett. "Do you think that I should seek professional advice?"

Everybody except me laughed and then everybody including me followed her over the bridge and towards the bar. I doubted that she would actually go inside and presumed that she was playing a tipsy, almost child-like game akin to knock-a-door-run. Yet as soon as she reached the entrance she disappeared through it. Not knowing what else to do we went in after. Then stood staring awkwardly at our feet.

All of the walls had been painted magnolia and then covered in photographs captured with a too bright flash and collaged together in a jumbled display reminiscent of the meal deals in a kebab shop. On our left was a doorway covered by a curtain made from plastic beads and in front of it a counter behind which a fat, bearded man was reading a science-fiction magazine.

Without looking up he said, "For women it's free."

His accent was Liverpudlian and so unexpected that for the first time I too laughed. I looked from him to the photographs, still laughing, then peered at the one nearest to me. A woman in a green rubber uniform was being penetrated by a man in a red rubber mask. Another woman in a matching outfit tugged at her nipples while she watched them.

A new thought occurred to me and I said abruptly, "But where are they from?"

"Eh?" said the man behind the counter.

"The women who work here. Who- who perform. Where are they from?"

"Everywhere," he gave me a curious look, "Or nowhere. They're international women of mystery."

"But what does that mean?"

But before he had time to answer I heard the tap and swoosh of the bead curtain. I realised that Scarlett had already gone inside and not wanting to be thought a prude I once again followed after her.

X

A young white woman knelt in the middle of a rotating stage. The boxy, pared-down design of her shirtdress could have alluded to a beautician, technician, or scientist as well as nurse had it not been realised in a shiny latex fabric. The top half was undone revealing two large sagging breasts that grazed the floor whenever she jerked forward while the skirt was pulled up as far as it would go so as to display the entirety of her ample bottom.

A young white man knelt behind her, thrusting. He was naked but for a plastic stethoscope that dangled down over his narrow chest. A row of spots ran across his jawline and a wispy moustache decorated his top lip. He looked like a student with an unexpectedly large penis. Also as if he might be high. Like the woman he groaned continually.

The other members of the audience consisted of three slightly greasy looking teenage boys and a pleasant looking middle-aged man who could easily have been their father. The teenage boys looked at the couple and sniggered. The middle-aged man massaged his crotch. Albion, Johnnie, Scarlett, and I resumed staring at the floor. And the real live fucking couple gazed into the middle distance united by the same glazed expression.

élégie

As soon as it finished we started drinking. We began with wine in a strange little bar where you could also eat schnitzel and old people sat in tobacco stained corners. Then we went back to the apartment and opened a bottle of brandy. Then once we had finished it we moved on to a strange smelling, purple liquid that although it clearly referred to some kind of fruit or berry none of us could be entirely sure which. I felt that it was only a matter of time before I vomited but also that I could not stop now.

"I think this is too much for an old bloke," said Albion, getting slowly to his feet, "I'm off to bed."

"Nooo!" and I grabbed his arm pulling him back towards me.

"Allegra! Please. You know that I'm meeting the Director tomorrow."

I let myself fall back onto the floor. Downed what remained of my drink then muttered 'spoil sport' into the empty glass.

"What?"

"I said- sorry. I was just being silly."

I was aware that Scarlett and Johnnie were exchanging glances in the background and I could smell the sweet ashy scent that was beginning to fill the air. I had grown so unused to my husband and now here I was expected not only to interact with him but to do so in front of the very people intended to prevent said interaction from occurring. I thought of the women in the cubicles and how they had wanted to ignore me. I thought of my face, my breasts, my labia and the ruby leaves that but a few hours earlier had floated on the canal. I thought in images all of which were already from the past until not knowing what else to do I reached for my phone. But I had no new messages. Then I looked around me for my laptop, which seemed to have disappeared . . .

"So I guess I'll see you in the morning then," said Albion.

"Oh yes, see you then," I said absently.

I pulled one of the cushions off the sofa and peered underneath it. Then did the same to the armchair. Finally I attempted to crawl under the coffee table. As I did so I realised that the apartment was not unlike our London home bar a brighter colour scheme and the addition of several technically well designed pieces of plastic furniture. For the first time I noticed that there was an orchid on the window sill, a detail that made me recall the first time that Johnnie and I had met. Once again I considered his comment about Romanticism. Having now given up on ever finding my laptop I wriggled out from underneath the coffee table and went over to the stereo. My drunken fingers prodded stupidly at the 'on/off' button but eventually yielded the desired resulted. I pressed 'play' on the track that I wanted, lay back, and waited. Slowly the tension began to build. A few seconds later the cello erupted and then kept on going until the whole room was immersed in the larva of Fauré and the best and the worst of his rising, booming, picturesque sorrow-

"Allegra what the fuck?!" shouted Johnnie.

"Allegra, *please!*" shouted Scarlett.

"Allegra!" shouted Albion, who had now reappeared in his underpants, "*Please.* I really need to sleep!"

Droom

I watched as Albion and the three drunk copies of him looked at me and then stroked the sides of their faces. I could see the linen creases that cut across their cheeks as well as how their stomachs overhung their waistbands. I saw that these Albions were fatter and older and more worn out than the one that I was used to, all of which filled me with a terrible and insatiable tenderness. I wanted to throw my arms around them and bury my head in their chests - but of course I didn't.

"You don't have to be sorry," the Albions said wearily, "just quieter."

I nodded guiltily then stood up. Sometimes I forgot how much taller other people were but now that we were all in such close proximity I could not help but feel it. Feel these other bigger bodies that knew my own so well. Of the way their sweat smelled, tasted even. Of our honeymoon in Athens and our current, present disconnect.

Turning to the Scarletts and the Johnnies I said, "I think that I might call it a night too."

I assumed that they nodded back. Then followed the Albions to the bedroom where they crawled under the covers.

I pulled back the top sheet and said, "I want us, all of us, to start a new life together, here, in Amsterdam. I want us, all of us, to be safe when the Brexit-apocalypse begins. But if I'm to protect you then I need to fix myself first, and that means that-"

"I need to sleep," muttered the Albion Chorus.

But I remained where I was whispering things that I meant at the time until my own heavy head began to droop. Then jerked awake again. Then drooping, drooping, dropping until I dropped down too pushing my face into the back of someone's neck and breathing into it.

Albion turned and murmured, "Allegra?"

But still not sure that this one was the right one I pretended to sleep.

Brown

It was early afternoon before Scarlett reemerged wearing the same tight, spangled jumpsuit as the night before. I could hear what I thought was Johnnie stirring also and not wanting to have to deal with him immediately ushered Scarlett out the door. We were too old to know that anything labelled as a coffee shop was actually aimed at marijuana smokers – a group to which neither of us believed that we belonged – and the Ethiopian flags that hung outside them merely confused us due to our not having encountered a single person of colour in the Netherlands thus far.

"But can't we just have coffee?" said Scarlett, and then nodding towards the brown café opposite, "Or else try there?"

"But you told me never to give a brown present."

"No, you told me. When I wanted to get something nice for Verity and you tried to put me off."

"Well, I wish that I'd succeeded," I said irritably, "she must be back from her retreat by now and still no call, unless that dangerous buffoon she calls a husband's started screening them. Now look," and I pointed to the place where Anker and I had stopped for take-out, "that almost looks like us."

Before Scarlett had chance to object I steered her inside and sat her down at the only free table. I scanned the menu very quickly and then ordered an unnecessary amount of food none of which I planned to eat while Scarlett kept on, silently opening and closing her mouth, as if gearing up for the revelation that I sensed was coming: namely that Verity was pregnant but had told her and not me first.

"I had hoped that she'd have been in touch herself by now," Scarlett said eventually and once again

I nodded, "and Hale promised me that he was going to send an email, but I suppose they've both been worried about your, you know, breakdown-"

"My what!?" but then I did my best to breath and what I hoped was calmly said, "I'm very sorry that Verity got the impression I was so . . . *unwell.* Why, whatever is the matter?"

"She . . ." and then more definitely, "She has cancer. At first it didn't look that bad. The doctors weren't sure whether or not she needed chemo, and being Verity she took that as a 'no'. And then she tried all sorts of things-"

"Juice cleanses?"

"Yes, exactly," and the Waitress placed two glasses of bright orange liquid on the table, "and acupuncture and Chinese herbs. But the cancer spread. It became more and more aggressive. And- and now she's in a hospice."

I watched as Scarlett's eyebrows came together in one sharp line and the brow above them furrowed. I had never seen her pull this expression before which, combined with her attempts to powder over the previous night's debauches, made it appear as though she were wearing an odd pierrot-the-clown style mask. I had often told myself that her reckless appearance and her reckless character were one and the same—a belief that always soothed me—and so to acknowledge that this might not really be the case was to acknowledge . . . *other sides.* And yet how could I find the room to see these things when it was already so hard to ascertain the perimeters of my own life? To see anything besides the mask that I myself had always worn? I tried to catch my breath but couldn't. Then covered my mouth with my good and bad hands.

"Could she-" and now it seemed as though everything all around us was slipping in and out of focus and as though everyone in the café was wearing a hideous costume, all of which were stolen from a box of children's toys, "Could she . . . ?"

"Yes of course. That's why people go to hospices."

Over

My Breakdown—inwardly I repeated the phrase. *My Breakdown*—and I kept on repeating it, constantly, disbelievingly, disgustedly for what little of Scarlett's visit remained. But then as soon as she and Johnnie had departed I remembered that I was still here and like it or not in the now and then I threw out—ripped out—that ugly little voice that had risen up from the depths of my childhood and left it to rot along with all the other, bloody items that didn't really need recycling.

And then into that space came *The Hospice* where sick people go to die. And it grew inside me until I became as empty as an empty bed in a hospice or a person who has nothing left that can be lost can be. Obviously I called Verity. And then when she didn't answer—most likely because the place that was not my breakdown did not allow for mobile phones—I called Hale. And then when he didn't answer I resorted to a voicemail on their landline:

"Hi Verity, Hi Hale, it's Allegra here, I'm calling because I just met with Scarlett and . . ."

And then I explained that I knew too now. And asked what I could do to help. And apologised first to Verity for my selfishness that was so awful and then to Hale because one extra beer after the concert was hardly a crime. But as I spoke these meaningful, sympathetic but ultimately empty words I began to understand that this same emptiness was also freedom from my own misery and chaos. Yes, I felt empty. I felt devoid. But more importantly I felt very, very calm and therefore capable. Unlike my friend I still had options. And this calm capability and these options were what would save me from going under now.

Garter

I went into the bathroom and very calmly tucked my skirt into my knickers. Then reached for Albion's razor and removed the blade. As I contemplated the sharp little sliver of metal I thought about how even though other people had done what I was now about to do to me on numerous occasions—some of them fairly recently— it had been over twenty years since I had done them to myself. Because for over twenty years I had been a self that on some level I had liked.

I held the blade between my thumb and index finger and with one leg on the bathtub carefully carved a 'V' and then a 'P' into my thigh before repeating the gesture until a row of these same letters encircled the top of my right leg creating a rusty, bloody garter. As I cut time stopped. I entered into an intense state of euphoria where my previous sense of calm became so vast and all encompassing that it was impossible to feel in any way separate from it. I thought of the circle of teethmarks on my shoulder (my wedding ring) and then the new letters (a friendship bracelet). I thought that my relationships had not been insignificant and that they had left their marks upon me. And then that my talent was not insignificant either, and had not yet gone.

Hot Chocolate

An hour or so passed during which I let this new, thin blood trickle and clot and hopefully aid what would soon become a scar. Then I rearranged my skirt, rinsed the blade and slid it back inside the razor. Then returned to the kitchen. There was no Sleepytime tea but there was some hot chocolate. The box was deep red with a picture of a ruddy cheeked nun wearing a large white wimple. I couldn't quite work out what the association was between the nun and the hot chocolate other than to make it seem less enjoyable but as there was nothing else on offer I put on a pan of milk and while waiting for it to boil called the Consultant's number. I had to hold for over ten minutes, which at no point upset me. Rather I made and enjoyed a hot chocolate that was richer than the packaging had let me to believe.

"Ms Le- I mean to say Allegra," said the Consultant's voice at last, "I hope there hasn't been any more . . . *complications*?"

"No, no, not at all. But when I first came to see you, I remember that you mentioned some 'riskier options'?"

"I . . ."

I could hear a strange, muffled coughing and imagined the Consultant looking beseechingly at the portrait of his wife. When he did begin to speak however I immediately forgot most of what he said bar the fact that yes, a second operation could indeed be performed and that yes, if it was successful then I would be successful again too . . .

". . . I feel that I should also add that although, when it does work, the recovery time is quicker, it often doesn't. And that when it doesn't it causes lasting harm," said the Consultant, "also, that it's very expensive."

"That's not a problem. I'm prepared to spend everything we have."

"And we would need to arrange an accident waiver."

"Perfectly fine. Go right ahead. Sign my life away."

"And you would still need to come and see me first. To review the current situation."

"But of course."

"And you'll be back in the UK . . . ?"

"As soon as an appointment is available."

"Okay," he sighed awkwardly, "I'll get Hayley to call you and set that up then." He sighed again. "And how long will you be here this time? In England?"

"I . . ."

And although still full of deep and wondrous calm this question sounded a distant siren. Albion I now realised would never be my England, because my England was the England of Elgar and my cello; a beautiful wooden case in which all of my deferments and projections and attachments were contained. My cello was me and my soul if I still had one-

I took another sip of hot chocolate, wiped away the brown moustache that it had left and then-

"Forever," I said very, very calmly.

In Waiting

There was still time before the Museum closed. I put my dirty cup in the dishwasher, went into the bedroom and pulled my travel-case out from underneath the bed.

I didn't see the point in taking any of my summer clothes—the ribbon-tie sandals for example—because I wouldn't need them in the near future and in the faraway I would be ready to adopt different fashions. Likewise, anything else that would leave too large and therefore noticeable a gap within the wardrobe that Albion and I now shared again stayed put. The numerous soaps and lotions remained in the bathroom for similar reasons. Also my toothbrush - too sure a sign that I was leaving. Yet the me to whom I was returning still demanded make-up and at least one piece of critically acclaimed, prettily bound literature for the journey because one never knew who one might encounter on it . . .

I folded each piece of clothing carefully and so that it would survive my travels without creasing. Then decanted my cosmetics into a transparent wash-bag and placed Albion's unread copy of *Adults in the Room* on top. I checked the weight of the case and convinced that all was as it should be very calmly pushed it back beneath the bed.

Etudes Boreales

The next day I decided that rather than feign sleep all morning I would accomplish more if I got up. So I did. I cleaned my teeth, brushed my hair, and pushed a tampon up my cunt that now bled from an unhappiness that was just plain ordinary.

"Goodbye!" I shouted at the bathroom inside of which Albion was showering.

"Whaa . . .?"

The sound of wet footsteps slapped across the tiles but I was already half way out the door. I walked briskly across the road and all the way to the end of it then stopped and twisted my wrist so that it prickled and clicked.

I carried on walking through the cyclists and along the canals, past Andreas Post and then stopped at a chocolatiers where I purchased several more boxes of hot chocolate. Ten minutes later I reached the Museumplein where I stood and stared at the contemporary art gallery. It was relatively early but I could see through the glass walls that both the bookshop and the cafeteria were already full. I had not yet had breakfast and the people inside were eating croissants. I considered joining them but after a moment's hesitation turned and headed towards the Concertgebouw instead. Again there was a café located in the glass fronted entrance hall although this time it was distinctly more old-fashioned looking and despite their being no books on sale people were actually reading them and not their phones.

I went up to the counter and ordered another hot chocolate. An old man sneaked a look in my direction then began whispering with an old woman. Outside I could see groups of students making their way into one museum or another and Anker sweeping through them on her bicycle. Then a girl whom I was sure that I recognised sat down at a neighbouring table. I scrutinised her face. It was the same pale oval as my own, but with the addition of Asian eyes and thin hair scraped back in the manner of those who thought less about their appearances than their art only her youth was enough to counteract this, one flaw and-

My Breakdown-

The Hospice-

Once again these terms began to hover at the threshold of my consciousness. I shut the door before they entered it however, and eager to keep them out reached for my phone. I checked my messages and saw that, sure enough, there was one from Hayley that included a list of potential appointment times. I replied that I was available for all of them as well as any cancellations and then put my phone back in my bag. As I did so I recalled Hui Yin's performance and then very calmly how it had lacked any real sensuality, and then more generally that it had lacked.

Her Initials

I finished my hot chocolate, picked up my bag and set off across the Museumplein, again, and towards the street of shops that ran behind it. A pair of high-heeled sandals—near identical to the one's that I had thrown away bar the fact that they were white—were displayed in one of the boutique windows. I entered, told the Assistant my size and then when she went to find them turned my attention to the only other customer and the matching dress of white Battenberg lace that she was holding up against her body.

The Assistant returned and I said, "The dress too."

The other customer brushed her hair to one side and looked at me. Again she had the same oval face that I did but this time it was accented by large, surgically enhanced lips that matched her large, surgically enhanced breasts. I thought of the Harley Street women and my own photoshopped face. I knew that I didn't want to be ageless or a doll with hard, smooth holes—like Mia's baby—but then that perhaps the only way to avoid these things was to have a baby that I didn't want . . . ?

I picked up one of the shoes and pretended to examine it while the other customer entered the changing room, and then when the Assistant returned with the dress I took it and followed after her. As she undressed I noticed that her pale, beige underwear matched. Her bra in particular fascinated me partly because the two taught balloons attached to her chest did not appear to need it and partly because this made it look like an extension of her body rather than an item designed to provide support.

I tapped her on the shoulder and said, "I really like your underwear."

"Oh, err thanks."

My gaze moved away from her bra and then settled on the 'J' and the 'P' that dangled from the thin gold chain around her neck.

She looked at me again and said, "My initials."

"But where did you get your underwear?" I persisted.

"Oh umm. . ."

She mentioned the name of another boutique further up the road. I thanked her and went back out into the shop. I paid for everything without looking at the price tags. Then I found the underwear boutique and bought two matching bra and pant sets. Then I walked back past the other boutiques and towards the Museumplein. I checked my phone and saw that there was one new message from Hayley. And then I thought about how in but a few hours time I would put my new dress and my new shoes on again, plus one of the new matching bra and pan sets, and go out and celebrate my birthday with my husband.

The Grand Amrath Hotel

The walls were a deep olive and the carpet a brooding maroon the same shade as the velvet upholstery. Outside it was still light and if one looked through the swirling cobweb pattern with which each window had been leaded then one could see seagulls swooping down across the harbour. Yet the tables were already lit with candles shining through their red containers and thus affording Albion, and presumably myself, a rosy and festive glow.

We had barely sat down when the Waitress came to take our order. She was nearing retirement and attired in the same well-pressed manner that all of the hotel staff but as she reached for her pad I noticed the words 'love' and 'hate' tattooed across her knuckles.

"A glass of merlot," said Albion.

"And for you lady?" said the Waitress.

There were no sounds other than our breathing and the faint clink of cutlery from the restaurant next door.

I looked at the bar menu then said, "Actually, what I'd really like is a hot chocolate."

The Waitress made a note of it then left. Outside a seagull flew into the glass, then dropped away. Inside the silence continued.

"I . . ." I said, eventually.

"Yes?"

"I don't know how this has happened . . ."

"How what has happened, Allegra?"

But before I could say more the Waitress returned with our drinks. I drank the entire cup of hot chocolate in one go. Then wiped my mouth on my white lace sleeve so that it looked as though a long brown skid mark stretched across it.

"I'm so sorry about what happened-" Albion began.

"But it wasn't your fault," I cut in quickly, "Hale promised to drive us, and if he hadn't wanted another beer, then you wouldn't have had to. And in his stupid car-"

"You can hardly blame Hale. I should been much more careful-"

"But it was your right of way-"

"But-"

"But nothing."

My voice was calm yet as firm and definite as a heavy shutter closing. It was imperative that we continue to keep the accident at bay and yet I knew that if this were to happen then it was I and not Albion who would have to take the lead.

I smiled my best smile and said, "So, what was the feedback from the exhibition?"

Albion looked confused.

"The exhibition?"

"Yes. Are there any reviews yet? Are they positive?"

"A few. And they're- but c'mon Allegra, since when have you been interested in art reviews?"

"I've always been interested in anything that relates to my husband's work," I said and laughed one of my most charming laughs before attempting once again to push the conversation forwards, "but do you think that the Museum are pleased? Will they want you to curate more shows?   Or offer you something permanent?"

"Well, that's a lot of questions . . ."

And yet there were even more to come. I would ask and Albion would answer until there was no room left for the past to intervene except that before I had chance to begin-

"I've booked a room," said Albion.

"But we have an apartment," and for the first time my voice was not quite so calm as it had been recently, "And I cleaned it. Again. This morning."

"But it's a special occasion."

"But . . ."

But nothing.

Suite No.5

The bedroom was also full of cobwebs. I drew the curtains over them and the velvet blocked out the last of the evening light. Then I went into the bathroom and surveyed the gold taps, the ice-white towels and the monogrammed laundry bag hanging on the door.

I returned to the bedroom and said, "It's very fancy."

Albion laughed.   He removed his jacket—a new one that I hadn't bought for him—and laid it across the armchair. In the background I could hear a couple in what I took to be the next room arguing. I glanced at the jacket's label, which was Dutch, and wondered, briefly, who had helped him to choose it.

I said, "The problem isn't our proximity to others, but the expectation that we will tolerate them."

Again Albion laughed. Then he went over to the stereo while I began taking off my clothes. I folded each item and placed them all on the stool beside the dressing table. A triptych of mirrors was attached to the top of it and as I moved I saw myself first in my new underwear—the colour of which made it appear as though I had neither pubic hair nor nipples—and then naked, which somehow made me appear more clothed. My profile, which I was not used to seeing, struck me as being incredibly haughty but I was pleased to note that the rest of my body was pretty much unchanged. My jawline was still taught. My breasts and bottom pert. My stomach a little more rounded but not yet flabby . . .

I went back into the bathroom and removed my tampon. As I did so Bach began to play and the grand yet gradual opening accentuated by the low open C string reached out to me and then flowed into me from underneath the door. I had always loved the first suite in particular while the sixth, the allemande, was the one that had played at our wedding. Yet it was the penultimate, the most resonant yet macabre suite that Albion had now chosen . . .

I returned to the bedroom. Apart from his jacket Albion was still fully clothed. I hung my head. Then went and laid it against his chest.

He stroked the back of my neck and said, "I've missed you."

Then took my face in his hands and raised it upwards kissing me on the mouth. And then he began to kiss my neck, my ears, and to run his hands across my breasts. The music grew louder, more insistent. The arguing in the next room was either drowned out by it or else stopped. I began to undo the buttons on his shirt working downwards from his collar to his belly. When I reached his buckle I undid it and pulled off his belt. Then I took hold of his right hand and began to wind the belt around it only he let his arm go limp, the leather strap uncoiling and then falling onto the ground between us.

"You sure you want this? Now?" said Albion.

"Of course." I picked up the belt and gave it back to him. "Why else would I be here?"

"But-"

"But nothing."

I knew that I needed to protect us both from any encroaching intimacies the effects of which would be even worse once I went away. Knowing this I walked over to the bed, lay down on my stomach and waited, another return to past behaviours designed to keep us safe from all the other things that this our present moment might otherwise become. In response I heard the cello wail and also a rustling sound, which I assumed must be Albion removing the rest of his clothes. I felt the blood filling my ears and my whole body tingling in anticipation-

And then the first lash came. And then the second. And with each of them and each of those that followed I knew without absolute certainty that my love was of the kind that ruined others. That it limped and flailed. That it was barren. And also that it always bled . . . On and on it went until there was only an endless, dizzying blankness into which I who was nothing poured everything . . . And then I was lost . . . And then everything that I was or had once been turned into nothing too.

Possession

I didn't know how long it had gone on for because I never did only that when I became aware of myself again Albion was inside me. I could tell that he was near to coming but then he stopped himself and grabbed me by the hair.

I whispered, "No, no, please don't."

But he forced me over so that I was lying on my back.

Again I said, "Please don't," and then, "Albion, please don't. *Please.*"

But he had pinned me down in such a way that I couldn't move my arms. All I could do was shake my head from side to side.

I shook it faster and faster, saying, "No, no, no," but very quietly so as not to disturb the couple in the room next door and then again, "No, no, please-"

But he pushed himself inside my mouth and so deep that I was choking. I could feel him banging against the back of my throat. All the air was being forced out of me and vomit was filling up the space where the air should have been. And then my whole body was buckling, coughing, and choking and he was rubbing his cum all over me, into my hair and across my face . . .

When I finally opened my eyes Albion was lying beside me kissing my neck, my ears, even my eyelids. Seeing him I began to weep – and then to rage. I was dimly aware that he had one arm raised against his face so as to avoid my blows but still I kept on - hitting and biting and scratching at this awful thing that lived inside me in the hope that it too would turn to stone and die-

My Breakdown-

The Hospice-

I shut my eyes and screamed out, "Satan!" and then even louder, "Satan! Satan! Satan!"

"But Allegra! Allegra *please!*"

"Satan!"

"But it's over!"

But still I couldn't stop myself. And so it continued: leaking and heaving and taking the devil in vain.

IV

Grey

Thick, heavy tears rained down upon the airport staff as they scurried back and forth across the runway. The British climate was not one that demanded joy or even misery, rather it allowed for every type of greyness, and although it seemed in many ways nonsensical to have developed Stockholm syndrome for a city other than Stockholm I was pleased to be home. 'Today is the first day of the rest of your life' proclaimed a sticker on the girl-beside-me's rucksack. Today is the first day of Autumn stated the screen on my phone and all too aware that time was passing I sent a text to Hayley confirming my appointment.

"It is now safe to switch on electronic devices," said the Stewardess.

I covered my phone with my scarf and while waiting for the other passengers to remove their bags from the overhead lockers took out my compact. My skin looked especially pale against my black, high-necked dress and my hair appeared both harshly coloured and dull. I ran the powder puff over my cheeks and forehead—and the dullness became more uniform —then drew on my eyes and lips. Then I stood up too trying not to wince as the ribbed, polyester seating rubbed against my thighs.

I passed through customs and baggage reclaim then stopped at a branch of WH Smiths. Stacks of newspapers covered with Union Jacks were piled up next to the till. 'The Great Brexit Hate Crime Myth' said the headline on one of them, 'Why EU MUST Give Us Good Deal' said another and then 'Berry Quits Bake-Off' on the front page of The Sun. I selected a bottle of sparkling water and drank it almost immediately. As the bubbles prickled against my cheek the same elegant Muslim woman that I had seen at the Opera swept by. This time however she was surrounded by body-guards and a personal assistant trailing endless Louis Vuitton luggage. A huge Mercedes SUV with blacked out windows pulled-up and the woman and her entourage got in. I could hear the click of camera Apps all around me and the hushed almost reverential buzz of gossip.

Risky

I took a taxi but the traffic was bad and I arrived at Harley Street much later than expected. I told the Driver to keep the engine running then ran up the steps and into the reception. I nodded at the Receptionist but before she could ask me to sign the book I had reached the Consultant's rooms and without knocking burst through the door.

"Allegra," he said, not getting up.

"Yes," and I felt something deep within me boring down into the ground. "Yes, it's me. I'm here."

"And how are you? After your Athenian adventures?"

"Well, I know that it must seem . . . *odd*," I began very earnestly, "but I felt so strange after the abortion- although I know that wasn't actually what it was. So hot and then so cold in the cemetery and then so alone and then-" and then realising that it was of course the damage to my wrist to which he had been referring I stopped, "But I was told there would be no further problems?" I said calmly.

"No, no, it hasn't aggravated anything . . ."

"But?"

"If you'd like to take a seat . . ."

I sat down trying not to wince as I did so while the Consultant reached inside his desk. He drew out a folder full of x-rays and placed one of them on top of a light-box.

"Now if we compare this with last time," and he drew out and then lit up another similar but more haphazard picture, "we can see that it is knitting together. However-"

"However?"

"However, *this* area," and he tapped a small section the shape of which resembled a broken heart, "has yet to fuse. That doesn't mean that it won't, in fact all our research suggests-"

"What percentage?"

"I'm sorry?"

"That it will heal fully. What percentage?"

"Well I don't know if it's wise to-"

"What percentage?"

"I don't want to be reductive, ideally-"

"I want to know what percentage. And I'm going to keep on saying, 'what percentage?' until you say what percentage. So if I were you I'd just say-"

"Fifty. About fifty percent."

The room was exactly the same as I remembered, as was my reflection in the mirror. I studied the lines around my mouth and eyes and then lost myself in the hair that lost itself in the wallpaper. Images of burning logs and falling leaves sprang to mind but without any of the poetic associations that such things usually evoked.

I looked back at him and said, "Then it's time to move onto the other, riskier options. I've brought the waiver form with me. It's signed."

"Allegra, I really feel obliged to point out that-"

"Could you love a cripple?" I cut in, but still very calmly.

"Well, I . . ." and then, "I'll make the arrangements."

The Selling of Indulgences

It was now nearing rush hour and in places the traffic had almost ground to a standstill. I looked at my phone and saw that I was becoming even later. Again I took out the compact and checked my appearance and again I decided that I looked pale and drawn. I thought about the difference between this reflection and the one in the Consultant's rooms—which was rosier but also more wrinkled—and wondered in each case whether to blame the mirror or the lighting . . .

The taxi slowed then pulled over. Outside the grey sky overhung the long red building opposite. A dull plume of smoke rose from one end and at the bottom of the picture the green, green grass of home. I brushed my hair one last time then pinched each cheek hard so as to make a bright spot in the centre. I took out my purse, removed several fifty pound notes and pressed them all into the Driver's hand.

Without making eye contact I said, "I can't bear being in debt."

"Thanks!" said the Driver, "But only if you're certain . . . ?"

I got out of the taxi and not knowing how to answer the question did not look back.

No. 1 in G major, K. 313

Unfortunately I had not missed any of the service. I could see Scarlett and Johnnie sat at the front of the Chapel and Ivan huddled a few rows behind them. Someone turned a decrepit sound-system on and a plaintive film-score started playing. Mentally I replaced it with the Royal Concertgebouw and Mozart and the gorgeous, tinkling concerto that Verity had loved, and sure enough the tears were soon coursing down my cheeks. As I wept I remembered my parents' funerals and how I had cried not for them but for my younger self and the great misfortunes that she had suffered in being born to two such inadequate people before once again crying for another me the fate of whom would soon be decided by an operation that might or might not work . . .

The music ceased. I stopped crying and a man in a clergy collar went and stood beside the coffin. His voice had a deep bass sound that allowed my mind to wander further into fantasies of what might lie ahead until I became so ensconced in them that when Verity's mother and then her sister took their turns I registered only the addition of a soprano and then a contralto. Yet as soon as Hale approached the lectern it was as though a metronome had started ticking, the rhythm so harsh and measured and accusatory that I was forced to remain on every level there. I put my hands over my ears and looked at Scarlett who had her head on

Johnnie's shoulder. Then at Ivan, who was turning a gold cigarette lighter in his hand. I pushed my fingers deep inside my ears and kept on pushing until it hurt and I began to worry about perforated eardrums but then the coffin started moving. All of the mourners fell silent and Verity's body trundled through a set of maroon velvet curtains the same shade as those at the Grand Amrath Hotel.

"We always wanted a family," Hale began again as the last section of the coffin—presumably feet —disappeared from view, "Verity would have made a wonderful mother . . ."

On the Nature of Daylight

Scarlett made room for me under her umbrella, which in keeping with the theme was black, and together we waited upon the scattering lawn like extra flecks of ash.

She put her free arm around my waist and said, "Do you need a lift? Hale offered to drive us," and we both looked in the direction of a large oak tree underneath of which a clumsy figure was standing with the rain running over him, "but then we thought it best if we took the keys, and, well, there's space in the car . . ."

I nodded but absently. In the distance I could see Ivan making his way towards us but kept on pretending that I hadn't right up until the point I felt his breath upon my throat. The thought that he had known about Verity's illness before I had filled me with hate as did his face which was now as pink and wet as boiled ham. Ignoring the heavy, laboured breathing beside me I continued to stare in silence at the oak. Five, ten, fifteen seconds went by and then-

"And how are you *feeling* Allegra?"

"Not well," I replied in a tone that I hoped matched the weather, "that awful music made me quite sick. Just because it's a funeral one shouldn't have to abandon good taste altogether and-"

"As an autonomous piece it failed," Ivan broke in, and his voice had the same strange resonance as the man in the clergy collar, "But today we are not autonomous. Today we have come together to mourn a great loss, an individual who-"

"We've already had the eulogy thank you."

"Allegra!" said Scarlett.

"Please," said Ivan.

I took out my compact, and checked my reflection in it then turned to Scarlett and said, "Actually, would you mind if I waited in the car?"

"If that's what you want . . .?"

She handed me Hale's keys, which were attached to a rainbow keyring, and I tried to walk away, only before I could do so Ivan grabbed my arm. Had I had time to consider my reactions then I would have refused to take the dirty cardboard bundle that he now pushed into my hands rather than allowing them to automatically clasp around it like a baby's, but unfortunately my time was running out, and what little of it remained was spent visualising an alternative future. Forced back into the present I now looked down and saw a packet of cigarettes with Ivan's lighter wedged inside, and then realised with genuine surprise that I had not yet seen him smoke. The thought that he might have had enough respect for Verity or at least the situation to refrain from this one vice would have touched me had I wanted to be touched. Only I didn't. So instead I nodded curtly and carried on walking.

Remains

Once more alone, I felt relieved, exhilarated even, that the arrangements for the second operation had been put in place but also dogged by the same nagging worry: what would I do if it didn't work?

"I'll kill myself," I said out loud.

I had said the same thing fairly often when I was younger but then the realisation not only that this was an option but an option that I in many ways wanted had made me feel afraid. But now I was comforted to think that should the worst happen then there would still be an escape. I unlocked the car, got in, and re-applied my lipstick, then and out of habit checked my messages. There was one from The_Saracens_79. I tapped on it and read:

For me, romance is anything which has a mystique attached to it, which fills one's soul with excitement, which restores one's hope in humanity. In the context of romantic love it is wanting to spend every moment with someone, becoming excited at the very mention of their name, or even rumour of them.

It may be a cliché, but being somewhere new with that special someone by my side, discovering a different place together is one of the most romantic moments I can think of.

A kiss under a tree in the rain. Another cliché, but very romantic nonetheless.

I think about lots of things in romantic terms: from great moments of discovery, to discussions over wine with friends.

Coming home to her (whoever she is) after a long day, but still wanting her the moment she appears. Also a realisation of just how much we need each other; played out through sex perhaps, but governed by love.

Fear is an instinctive reaction to a perceived danger and expectation of pain or injury. This encompasses anything from jumping back from a snake in the grass, to ending a relationship because one is afraid of falling in love and getting hurt (another cliché?).

As a teenager I feared all sorts: everything from not growing enough body hair to wondering if I would ever recover from my early, hormone-fuelled infatuations. I suppose that that ties into fear of the opposite sex, because anything precious contains the fear of loss within it (as above!).

It's hard for me to talk about fear of either parent because it was never consciously present, except for times when I had been extremely naughty and was expecting some kind of physical punishment; usually just a slap on the back of my legs. But I suppose I carried some psychological fears regarding them. I was afraid of never living up to their high standards, which, sometimes, I thought were arbitrary and unfair, although I realise now were just their way of trying to make me push myself - to become the best I could be.

I don't know much about art, but the painting that immediately springs to mind is Rossetti's Veronica Veronese. *The way it portrays nature*

*and human achievement, and their being in
harmony with one another is pretty special.*

*My favourite piece of music is an instrumental
by Max Richter - a wonderful, bitter-sweet
melody, and also the theme to one of my
favourite science-fiction films.*

*When I look in the mirror I see room for
improvement. Yes, in some ways physically, but
more with regards to my career, to being a
friend, a father, a son, etc. There are many
things in my life that make me feel insecure.*

*What do I hear when something wonderful
happens? I'm not sure I hear anything at all. I
feel joy when it does, either to me or someone I
know, or just out there in the world. The details
are hardly ever relevant; I am just happy that
something good has occurred.*

Outside the rain beat down until it completely
obscured the view from Hale's car and I couldn't see or
hear anything else. The smell of diesel was
overpowering and the smell of smoke was in my hair. I
flicked Ivan's lighter, letting the flame burn my fingers
and pictured the curtains parting as Verity's coffin
rattled through them and then my birthday at the Grand

Amrath Hotel. I thought of the bright orange juice that I had drunk in Athens and in Amsterdam, the welts on my thighs and then finally my cello, my other spruce and maple self, also burning.

Acknowledgments

Thank you to Natasha Zielazinski for her insights regarding the life of a cellist (and to Jane Cheadle for putting us in touch). Thank you to Tom Cowdrey, Andreas Korte, Lucy Gayden, Keith Davis, Elinor Cooper, James Harding, Tessa Baird, Bea Turner, Caterina Lewis, and Mimei Thompson for sharing their reactions to different musical compositions (and allowing me to steal bits from them). Thank you to Phoebe Blatton for introducing me to *The Dialogues of the Carmelites*. Thank you to James, Andy, and Simon for giving me permission to use, and adapt, their emails. Thank you to MOIST (who published me). Thank you to the Arts Council (who funded me). Thank you to everyone else that I usually thank.

About the Author

Susan Finlay is a writer and artist. She is the author of three poetry pamphlets: *Indole* (2019), *The Unruly Glove, the Green Bum and the Sickly Trickle* (to accompany an exhibition by Zoe Williams, 2018), and *Sex and the City 2* (2017), and three previous novels: *Objektophilia* (2020), *Our Lady of Everything* (2019), and *Arriviste* (2007). In 2020 she was writer-in-residence at the Freud Museum, London. She lives in the UK and Berlin

My Other Spruce and Maple Self is the second book in MOIST's first season. The other titles in 'A Trilogy of Alienation' are:

Equilibrium by Tonino Guerra

Florilegia by Annabel Dover